Pillow Tales I

Parent-Child
20 Bedtime Stories

5 minutes
stories

Ingram Hart

Pillow Tales I

Parent-Child
20 Bedtime Stories

5 minutes
stories

Ingram Hart

Cover design and illustration by: Midjourney.com & Andri Gylfason

From the Author

Dear Reader,

Welcome to this enchanting world of bedtime stories, where the magic of words and the warmth of a parent's love intertwine to create cherished memories. As the author of these tales, I am delighted to invite you and your child on a journey through the pages of this book, where the power of storytelling comes to life.

In our fast-paced world, where days seem to fly by, there is something remarkable about the quiet moments before bedtime. These moments are precious when a child is tucked snugly into bed, ready to embark on a journey to dreamland. They are moments of connection, bonding, and love. These moments lay the foundation for a lifelong love of reading and, more importantly, a profound relationship between parent and child.

Bedtime reading is not just about putting a child to sleep; it's about awakening their imagination, fostering empathy, and building a strong emotional bond. It's a chance for a parent to step into characters' shoes, explore far-off lands, and dive into adventures with their child, all from the cozy confines of a bedtime nook.

This book is a testament to the power of these moments. Each story within these pages is crafted with the hope that it will transport you and your child to a world where anything is possible. Whether it's a whimsical adventure, a lesson in kindness, or a tale of friendship, these stories are designed to spark conversations, nurture curiosity, and fill your child's dreams with wonder.

As a father, I have experienced the joy of bedtime reading with my children. I have witnessed firsthand the sparkle in their eyes as we've embarked on journeys together and the magic that unfolds when a story becomes a bridge between generations. I sincerely hope this book will serve as a bridge for you and your child, a bridge that brings you closer and opens up a world of possibilities.

So, as you embark on this adventure through the world of bedtime stories, remember that these moments are not just about the words on these pages but the love and connection you share with your child. Treasure these moments, for they are fleeting, yet they are the stuff that childhood memories are made of.

May this book become a cherished part of your nightly routine, a source of comfort, and a catalyst for dreams. May it remind you of the importance of bedtime reading, not only in your child's growth but also in the deepening of your relationship.

With warmest wishes,

Ingram Hart

Contents

Story 1

Harrison the Hedgehogs Starry Night Adventure"

In a cozy little home beneath some prickly bushes, there dwelled a friendly hedgehog named Harrison. Harrison was a bashful little creature who found happiness in the small things in life. He liked snuggling up in a comfy heap of leaves, munching on yummy bugs, and gazing at the glittering stars in the dark night sky.

On a cold and crisp night, as Harrison wrapped himself into a cozy ball for sleep, something truly amazing happened. A bright shooting star streaked across the dark, velvet-like sky, grabbing his attention. Harrison uncurled himself and gazed up at this incredible sight in the sky, his eyes wide with wonder.

"Oh, how truly amazing!" he whispered to himself.

Harrison looked up at the night sky, full of wonder. And then, a magical thing happened! A bright star in the sky seemed to twinkle just for him. It didn't stay up high for long; it slowly came down and landed in a clearing not far away. Harrison's heart started to beat faster because he was so curious.

Gently and quietly, he reached out and inched closer to the mysterious visitor. What happened next was truly amazing! Right there, in front of him, was a tiny, shining creature. It wasn't just any creature; it was a little star sprite named Stella. Harrison was so shocked; he couldn't believe what he was seeing!

Stella was like nothing Harrison had ever seen before - a bright being with a shiny, star-like glow around her. She told Harrison that she had fallen from the night sky by mistake and needed help to get back home. Harrison was fascinated by Stella's sparkling presence and wanted to help her find her way back.

Being a very kind hedgehog, he quickly said yes to helping Stella on her trip among the stars. Their adventure began as they set off together through the forest, with the moonlight shining brightly above them.

Their first stop was a calm pond, where the water reflected the sparkling stars above. Frogs and fireflies made beautiful music as they floated across the pond on a lily pad raft, feeling like they were soaring through the night sky.

After that, they went into an ancient and special place in the forest, where wise owls told stories about faraway stars and galaxies, and elderly fireflies made pictures of stars in the sky using their glowing lanterns.

Harrison and Stella kept going on their exciting adventure, and they reached a magical meadow that was glowing in the moonlight. In this special meadow, they danced beautifully with tiny fireflies, just like they were in a cosmic dance show. Every time they twirled and spun around, they made their very own starry patterns on the grass, which was all covered in sparkly dewdrops. Their journey was filled with enchantment and wonder!

As the night went by, Harrison and Stella continued their journey through the forest, climbing higher and higher until they reached the tallest hill. From there, they could see the night sky filled with countless

twinkling stars, stretching out as far as they could see. Stella's glow became even brighter, and it was clear that she was getting ready to go back to where she truly belonged, up in the sky with the stars.

Harrison looked at his new friend, feeling both happy and a little bit sad. He said, "I'll miss you, Stella," and a tiny tear rolled down his cheek.

Stella smiled with love and said, "I'll miss you a whole bunch, Harrison." She talked really nicely, "But don't forget, whenever you look at the shiny stars in the night sky, I'll be up there with them, taking care of you and sending lots and lots of love to you." Stella gave Harrison a big hug, and he felt very happy and safe.

Harrison felt comforted by Stella's words. He knew that even when they were apart, they could still share the magic of the starry night sky. Stella's words filled his heart with happiness as he set off on his

14

adventure, knowing that a piece of Stella would always be with him in the twinkling stars above.

With a bright and dazzling burst of light, Stella went up into the night sky, leaving Harrison standing on the hill. He stared up, feeling his heart filled with amazement and a touch of magic as he watched his dear friend become a part of the glittering stars. The hill seemed like a special place where dreams could come true.

From that day on, Harrison really liked the night sky a lot. He would often snuggle up under the stars, feeling like they were his special friends. When the sky was clear, and he saw a shooting star, he would make a wish. He believed that Stella, his starry buddy, was shining up in the sky, winking at him. And this made him feel very happy. So, Harrison and Stella's friendship grew stronger with each starry night, and they had many wonderful adventures together.

Deep in the middle of the forest, under the shiny stars at night, Harrison the hedgehog had discovered a friendship that was even more special than anything he could imagine. This friendship was so magical that it went beyond the Earth and touched the incredible beauty of the universe.

From that day on, Harrison kept living his quiet life in the forest, but he always remembered that the starry sky was his forever friend. He knew that special friends could be found in surprising places, like among the twinkling stars in the night sky. Harrison's heart was filled with happiness because he had a friend that would never fade away, no matter how far it twinkled in the endless universe. And with his starry friend, he would have many more adventures and discover even more amazing things in the world and beyond.

The end.

Story 2

Olivia's Magic Garden

Once upon a time, in a cute, tiny cottage filled with sunshine, tucked away on the edge of a lively village, there dwelled a happy young girl named Olivia. Olivia was full of energy, with a heart that shined like the sun, and she felt as free as a bird in the wind. But most of all, she cherished her special, enchanted garden with all her heart.

Olivia's garden was truly one-of-a-kind. It wasn't like any other garden you've ever seen. In her magical garden, flowers talked quietly to each other, butterflies twirled and danced to the sweet songs of hummingbirds, and fireflies turned the nighttime into a beautiful painting of sparkling lights. Every day, something enchanting and extraordinary happened in Olivia's special garden, making it a place of endless wonder and joy.

One bright and sunny morning, while Olivia was taking care of her amazing garden, she discovered something truly special. Right there, among the beautiful flowers, was a tiny, shimmering seed. It was glowing with a magical light that made her heart feel full of awe and amazement. Olivia couldn't believe her eyes.

Without a moment's hesitation, Olivia delicately planted the mystical seed into the soft, fertile soil of her garden. Olivia took good care of it by giving it water and singing lovely songs to it every day. As time passed, something wonderful happened – the seed started to grow little by little.

When the time was right, something amazing appeared. Right in the middle of Olivia's garden, there grew a sunflower that was truly unique. It stood proudly and tall, unlike any other sunflower. Its petals were as bright and shiny as pure gold, and it had the happiest face that seemed to spread warmth all around. It was a sunflower like no other, and it made Olivia's garden a very special place.

The sunflower looked at Olivia and said, "Thank you for making me grow and come to life." Its voice was as gentle as a soft breeze that whispers through the leaves of trees. Olivia smiled back at the sunflower, feeling grateful for the magical flower in her garden. She knew that this sunflower was no ordinary flower, and their friendship was just beginning to bloom.

Olivia quickly gave her new friend a special name - Sunny. From that moment on, they were always together, like two peas in a pod. With Sunny beside her, Olivia's garden turned even more enchanting. Beautiful flowers covered the ground with lots of different colors, and happy birds sang the most delightful tunes for them to hear.

But as the seasons changed and the days got colder, Olivia saw something worrying happen. Sunny's petals started to bend down, and his once-shiny face didn't look as happy anymore. Olivia was concerned about her friend Sunny.

Olivia was filled with sadness. She loved Sunny so much and didn't want to lose him. But inside her heart, she also felt strong and courageous. So, she made a brave decision. She decided to go on a big adventure. Her mission was to find the wise old tree that lived deep in the heart of the forest, where magical secrets were hidden.

With Sunny happily sitting on her shoulder, Olivia went on a big adventure into the forest, where the very old trees shared their special secrets through soft whispers. Olivia told her story to the wise old tree, and the tree listened carefully. Then, as a special gift, the tree gave her a little crystal that sparkled like tiny stars in the night sky.

The wise old tree said, "This crystal has the forest's magic inside it. Plant it beside Sunny, and it shall help him bloom even through the coldest of winters." And the wise old tree smiled, knowing that the power of nature and friendship could make even the coldest times feel warm and bright.

Feeling very thankful for the forest's wisdom, Olivia went back home. She planted the crystal next to Sunny, and something amazing happened. She watched with wide eyes as Sunny's droopy petals started to shine brightly with their golden color again. Olivia was so happy to see her friend looking so beautiful once more.

Thanks to the crystal's magic, Sunny didn't just make it through the tough winter; he bloomed even more beautifully when spring

arrived. Olivia's garden turned into a truly magical place that made everyone in the village amazed. Children from all over came to play in the garden where the flowers could talk, and the butterflies danced around joyfully. It was a place filled with happiness and wonder.

But you know what was really, really special? It was the super-duper friendship between Olivia and Sunny. They were best pals, and they did

everything together. They laughed, told each other exciting tales, and had so much fun taking care of their magical garden. It was like a dream come true!

And that's how the wonderful story ends, my young friends. Olivia and Sunny, in their lovely cottage filled with sunshine, kept taking care of their magical garden. They showed everyone that amazing friendships can be discovered in the most surprising spots.

As days turned into weeks, and weeks into months, their garden blossomed even more. People from the lively village nearby would often visit, and they too learned about the beauty of friendship, kindness, and the magic of nature.

Olivia and Sunny's garden became like a living book of love and goodness. It proved that no matter where you look, you can find extraordinary friendships if you keep your heart open. And as the seasons changed, their garden continued to flourish, reminding everyone of the enduring magic that surrounds us every day.

The end.

Story 3

Benny and the Magical Kite

Once upon a time, in a busy town tucked snugly among big, bumpy hills, there lived a curious boy named Benny. Benny had bright eyes that sparkled like the morning sun, and a heart full of wonder that seemed to overflow every day. But what he loved most was flying kites.

Benny had a collection of kites, each one more colorful and whimsical than the last. His favorite was a bright red kite with a long, rainbow tail. It was a gift from his grandfather, who had taught Benny everything he knew about kite-flying.

One bright morning, Benny thought it would be fun to bring his favorite kite to the biggest hill in town. When a strong wind blew, and Benny giggled, he made the kite fly high in the sky. The kite danced and spun around with the white clouds, adding lots of pretty colors to the wide, blue sky.

As Benny watched his kite, he couldn't help but wonder about the world beyond. He imagined flying with his kite, high above the hills and rivers, visiting distant lands filled with adventures and surprises.

To his big surprise, Benny felt like his kite could understand what he wanted. It pulled on the string a little bit, telling Benny to come along. Benny's heart filled with happiness, and he started to run, with his kite showing him where to go.

They flew up high, leaving the town behind. Benny was amazed as everything changed. He saw big forests with singing birds, shiny rivers with jumping fish, and endless fields of colorful flowers.

But just as Benny was beginning to wonder where his kite would take him next, they descended gently into a magical forest. Trees with leaves of gold and silver reached out to welcome him, and the air was filled with the sweet scent of blooming flowers.

In this enchanted forest, Benny met a friendly fox named Felix, a wise old owl named Oliver, and a playful rabbit named Rosie. They told him tales of the forest's wonders and invited him to join their games and adventures.

Felix, the fox, was an expert at hide-and-seek, disappearing among the trees with a flash of his bushy tail. Oliver, the owl, shared stories of ancient wisdom, teaching Benny about the stars and the secrets of the night. Rosie, the rabbit, led Benny on a merry chase through fields of clover, his giggles echoing through the forest.

As the day turned to night, Benny knew he had to return home. With a tug on the string, his kite obediently carried him back to the hill where his journey had begun. He landed softly on the grass, surrounded by his new forest friends.

Benny said thanks to his magical kite and waved goodbye to the magical forest. With happy memories in his heart, he went back to his busy town and told everyone about his amazing adventure.

From that day on, Benny's kite was not just a colorful toy; it was a gateway to a world of wonder and friendship. He continued to fly it on sunny days, knowing that it held the promise of endless adventures and the magic of making new friends.

In the busy town, with big hills all around, Benny and his kite flew up high. They showed everyone that amazing adventures can start with just a string and a curious heart.

Benny's adventures with his magical kite became legendary in his town. Kids from all over would come to a big hill, and they would look up in the sky. They wanted to see Benny's colorful kite flying way up high, like it was dancing with the clouds.

Whenever Benny's kite went up in the air, it felt like it brought a little piece of magic from the forest with it.

One breezy afternoon, as Benny was flying his kite, a group of children approached him. They had heard the tales of his incredible adventures and wanted to know if his kite could take them on a journey too.

Benny smiled and gave the kite string to an excited child. "Hold tight and imagine something amazing," he told the child. When the child held the string, the kite flew up, and all the children went on a magical adventure.

They flew over pretty fields with colorful flowers and went past clear streams where magical animals played. They found a secret place where fireflies danced like twinkling stars.

Benny was happy as he saw the children feeling the same wonder, he did on his first adventure. It's like the magic forest gave his kite its enchantment, so others could discover its secrets too.

As the sun began to set, Benny helped guide the children back to the hill. They landed safely, their faces filled with wonder and gratitude. Benny knew that his kite had brought joy to not only him but to a new generation of adventurers.

News about Benny's magical kite traveled everywhere, and kids from nearby towns and villages came to join the fun. Benny became a beloved person, not just in his town, but in the whole area. He taught the kids to love nature, see its beauty, and value the friends they made on their trips.

The magical forest, once a secret, now had lots of visitors. It loved the kids' laughter and curiosity. Benny's kite showed them the way as they explored its wonders.

Benny's kite was a sign that childhood is magical, and the world has amazing things to find. Benny, with his curious heart and bright eyes, kept inspiring new adventurers. He showed that great journeys start with a simple string and a curious heart.

And so, in the busy town tucked snugly among big, bumpy hills, Benny and his kite continued to soar into the sky, spreading the joy of discovery and the magic of friendship to all who dared to dream.

The end.

Story 4

Mia and the Enchanted Paintbrush

Once upon a time, in a cozy village nestled near a huge mountain, there was a creative girl named Mia. Mia had bouncy, curly hair that danced in the wind, and her eyes twinkled with never-ending wonder. But what made Mia the happiest of all was painting.

Mia's room felt like an enchanted treasure chest, brimming with paints, brushes, and canvases in every dimension. She spent her time capturing the beauty of the world, making paintings that burst with life on her special stand. Her art had a magical power, taking anyone who looked at it to far-off places and lost dreams.

One bright morning, as Mia was busy exploring the attic of her snug little cottage, she happened upon a dusty old paintbrush. But this was not just any paintbrush; its bristles sparkled like moonbeams, and its handle was covered in intricate designs that looked like they held a tale. It seemed to have a magical air about it as if it held a secret only Mia could discover.

Mia took her special brush and dipped it into her rainbow paints. She painted on her canvas, and wow! The colors came alive, dancing and swirling. Her canvas turned into a real place. Trees moved their leaves, birds flew high, and flowers danced in the breeze. Mia's imagination made the world come alive!

Word of Mia's extraordinary gift spread like wildfire throughout the village. People came from distant places to see her enchanting art. Mia painted scenes of incredible beauty and heartwarming tales, each one more enchanting than the previous. Her paintings filled everyone who saw them with happiness and awe.

Yet, Mia soon learned that her newfound ability carried important duties. She knew that her art could mend hurts, ignite dreams, and encourage change. And so, she committed herself to using her gift to make her village and the world a better place.

Mia painted murals that celebrated togetherness and differences, drawing her community nearer. She crafted landscapes that urged folks to remember how vital it was to protect nature, motivating them to care for the environment. With her brush, she wove tales of courage, love, and optimism, igniting a spark of hope in the hearts of everyone who gazed upon her creations.

As the days turned into years, Mia's fame as a magical artist grew, but she remained humble and committed to her purpose. Her enchanting paintings didn't just change her village; they touched hearts around the world. Mia's legacy lived on, a reminder that creativity and art could work magic, one brushstroke at a time. In that charming village beneath the towering mountain, Mia's story became a cherished legend, inspiring many to find their magic within the canvas of life.

With her magical paintbrush, Mia painted enchanted forests where

talking animals shared stories, castles where friendly dragons guarded treasures, and underwater kingdoms where colorful fish sang songs of the sea. She shared her magical creations with her friends and the entire village, filling their hearts with wonder.

On one fateful day, while Mia painted a bustling city scene with cars racing along colorful streets, something truly extraordinary occurred. A tiny, painted character leaped out of her canvas and came to life. This little being was a playful and mischievous paintbrush sprite known as Spark.

Spark shared that the enchanted paintbrush was far from ordinary; it served as a gateway to a world of magic and excitement. Mia and Spark began a remarkable adventure through her paintings, exploring the imaginative realms she had brought to life.

They ventured deep into her ocean realm, soared through her

enchanted forests, and even enjoyed tea parties with the whimsical creatures from her meadows. Mia's creative world had become a tangible, magical land, and she was the artist-adventurer at its core.

But as days turned into nights, Mia began to miss her village and her friends. With a heavy heart, she decided it was time to return home.

With a final dip of her enchanted paintbrush, Mia stepped out of her last painting and back into her cozy cottage. Spark promised to visit her whenever she needed a bit of magic in her life.

Mia continued to paint, but now with a newfound appreciation for the magic that could be found in the everyday world. Her paintings were filled with the beauty of her village, her friends, and the adventures she had experienced.

And so, in the picturesque village nestled at the foot of a great mountain, Mia continued to create and imagine, reminding everyone that with a touch of magic and a heart full of creativity, the ordinary could become truly extraordinary.

Mia came back to her village, and everyone was so happy! They threw a big party for her. Mia had been on amazing adventures, and she found a magical world.

Her friends and neighbors thought Mia's stories were super cool. They also loved her paintings even more now. Her paintings didn't just have fun things from her imagination, but they also had stories from her travels. Everyone in the village loved hearing all about her adventures and looking at her magical paintings.

Mia became a famous artist and adventurer. People from all over the place came to see the magic of her special paintbrush. They wanted to see the wonderful world her paintings made real.

The village turned into a super busy and creative place. Artists and dreamers came from all around to get inspired by Mia's amazing art. It was like a big party of imagination!

Mia's village was full of life, and so were her friendships. She asked her old pals to come paint with her on adventures. They made lots of magical worlds together.

Mia's special paintbrush wasn't just her secret anymore. It made everyone happy and gave them lots of good ideas.

In all the fun, Mia never forgot Spark, the playful paintbrush sprite who showed her the enchanting world. Spark kept his promise and visited Mia sometimes, adding magic to her everyday life. He reminded her that ordinary things could be just as special as extraordinary ones.

The end.

Story 5

Lucy and the Starlit Adventures

In a cozy little cottage tucked away in a charming village, there lived a young girl named Lucy. Lucy had a heart that sparkled as brightly as the stars in the night sky, and a spirit filled with endless curiosity. But what she loved most was gazing at the stars.

Every night, Lucy would climb onto her roof, where she had placed a cozy blanket and a telescope. With her eyes fixed on the heavens, she would lose herself in the mysteries of the night, dreaming of far-off galaxies and distant constellations. Her roof had become her own private observatory, a place where her imagination could take flight.

Once on a night when the moon was shining brightly, Lucy looked through her special telescope. And guess what? She saw something really amazing! A star moved super-fast across the sky, and it left a shiny trail of star dust behind it. Lucy felt so happy and excited that her heart went thump-thump! She closed her eyes and made a wish, just like she always did when she saw a shooting star.

But this time, something incredible happened. The shooting star seemed to pause in its descent and then gently landed in Lucy's outstretched hand. It was a tiny, radiant star named Stella.

Stella's light shimmered with a soft, gentle glow. She explained that she had fallen from the night sky and needed help finding her way back. Lucy, with her heart full of kindness, agreed to help Stella on her celestial journey.

Lucy held Stella in her hand and wished on the star. Suddenly, they flew up into the night sky. They zoomed past shiny galaxies and colorful clouds. Lucy thought the universe was amazing and full of wonders.

Their journey took them to distant planets, where they met alien creatures with tales of their own. They traveled through asteroid fields and danced among the rings of Saturn. Stella's light guided them safely through the cosmic seas, and Lucy's curiosity knew no bounds.

As the night went on, Lucy and Stella found a magical garden in the sky. The flowers there were so bright and pretty. Each flower had a special story. Lucy picked a tiny glowing flower and put it in her hair to remember their big adventure.

But as the night got late, Lucy knew it was time to go home. She made one more wish on Stella, and they floated back to her rooftop. Lucy held Stella and looked at the starry sky. She said, "I'll miss you, Stella," feeling thankful and a little sad.

Stella smiled warmly. "And I will miss you too, Lucy. But remember, whenever you gaze at the night sky, I'll be among those stars, watching over you."

With a brilliant burst of light, Stella returned to the night sky, leaving Lucy standing on her rooftop, her eyes shimmering with tears of both joy and longing.

From that night forward, Lucy saw the world with new eyes. She no longer needed Stella's physical presence to feel the magic of the universe. She had discovered that the real magic was not just in the stars above but also in the kindness and wonder that lived within her heart.

Lucy shared her tales of starlit adventures with her family and friends, inspiring them to look up at the night sky with a sense of wonder and connection to the cosmos. They would often gather on her rooftop, each taking turns looking through the telescope, and sharing stories of their own dreams.

In Lucy's lovely cottage, she kept looking at the stars. She knew each star had a story, and the universe was full of amazing adventures. She also remembered Stella was up there, watching over her, reminding her that small acts of kindness can lead to big journeys. Lucy's heart stayed as happy as the stars, and she felt like a part of the magic in the night sky, forever connected to its wonder.

As the years passed, Lucy's love for the stars grew stronger, and she became a renowned astronomer, discovering new celestial wonders and sharing her knowledge with the world. She named a newly discovered star cluster in honor of Stella, ensuring that her friend's memory would shine on for generations to come.

Lucy's adventures were no longer limited to the night sky. She traveled the world, spreading her message of wonder and kindness, encouraging people of all ages to never stop dreaming and to always look up at the stars with hope in their hearts.

Lucy's village became a hub of celestial exploration, with stargazing festivals and astronomy clubs flourishing. She dedicated herself to educating the next generation of young astronomers, teaching them to reach for the stars and explore the endless possibilities of the universe.

And so, Lucy's legacy extended far beyond her charming village. Her story of friendship with Stella and her passion for the stars inspired countless others to seek out their own starlit adventures. The night sky, once a canvas of mystery, became a tapestry of dreams and hope, with Lucy's bright star at its center, shining as a beacon of kindness and wonder.

In every heart she touched, Lucy left a little piece of the magic she had experienced on that fateful night. Her cozy cottage remained a gathering place for kindred spirits, where stories of exploration and discovery filled the air, and the stars above twinkled with the promise of new adventures.

As Lucy looked up at the night sky, she knew that Stella was still out there, watching over her and the countless others who had been touched by their friendship. And as long as there were dreamers and stargazers, the legacy of Lucy and Stella's starlit adventures would continue to shine brightly, illuminating the path to endless wonders in the universe and within our own hearts.

The end.

Story 6

The Tale of Sammy and the Whimsical Forest

In a quaint little cottage at the edge of a vibrant village, there lived a young boy named Sammy. Sammy had a mop of unruly hair that seemed to have a mind of its own, and a heart that was always brimming with curiosity. But what he loved most was exploring the mysteries of the forest.

The forest near Sammy's home was like no other. It was known as the Whimsical Forest, a place where magic and wonder flowed like a gentle stream. The trees whispered secrets, the flowers sang sweet melodies, and the animals wore hats and scarves in bright, cheerful colors.

On a bright and sunny morning, Sammy went on an adventure into the Enchanted Forest. While he was exploring deeper into the forest, he found something really amazing - a special acorn that was glowing like magic. It sparkled with a light from another world, and when Sammy picked it up, he suddenly felt full of energy and excitement!

Curious and adventurous as ever, Sammy decided to plant the acorn in a small clearing he had discovered. He watered it with care and sang a cheerful tune to it every day. To his amazement, the acorn sprouted into a whimsical tree unlike any other.

The tree had leaves that changed color with the seasons, and its branches swayed to unheard melodies. It seemed to have a personality of its own. Sammy named it Whisk, for it whisked him away into delightful adventures.

Sammy and his best friend Whisk went on a big adventure in the Whimsical Forest. They met animals that could talk and tell tricky riddles. They found secret paths that took them to magical meadows, and they even had tea parties with fairies who sprinkled them with special stardust. It was a really fun journey!

Every day brought new wonders and surprises. Sammy and Whisk discovered sparkling streams where fish told tales of underwater castles, and they explored towering mushroom groves that served as homes for friendly gnomes.

But as the seasons changed, and winter's chill began to fill the air, Sammy noticed something troubling. Whisk's leaves began to wither, and its vibrant colors faded. Sammy's heart sank, for he didn't want to lose his magical friend.

Determined to save Whisk, Sammy set off on a journey to find the Wise Old Owl of the Whimsical Forest. With the owl's ancient wisdom, he hoped to discover how to restore Whisk's magic.

Through moonlit glades and twinkling firefly paths, Sammy and Whisk reached the heart of the forest, where the Wise Old Owl perched atop a majestic oak tree. The owl listened to Sammy's tale and spoke in riddles that seemed to float on the breeze.

"The magic of Whisk lies in the laughter of children and the wonder of the world," the owl said. "To restore its magic, you must share its tales and wonders with the villagers."

Sammy returned to his village with Whisk, and together, they shared the stories of their whimsical adventures with the villagers. Sammy painted vivid pictures of the enchanted forest, and the children listened with wide-eyed wonder.

As the villagers heard about the talking animals, the stardust tea parties, and the sparkling streams, they were filled with a sense of enchantment. And in their hearts, they too began to believe in the magic of the Whimsical Forest.

As the stories spread, something extraordinary happened. Whisk's leaves began to regain their vibrant colors, and its branches swayed to the joyful laughter of children. It was as if the forest itself had come to life in the hearts of the villagers.

And so, in the quaint little cottage at the edge of the vibrant village, Sammy and Whisk continued their adventures, reminding everyone that the most magical places could be found in the imagination, and the greatest adventures were those shared with a friend.

As the seasons turned, Sammy and Whisk's bond with the forest grew stronger. They discovered even more enchanting secrets hidden within the Whimsical Forest. One day, they stumbled upon a hidden glade filled with luminous fireflies that created a breathtaking display of light every night. Sammy and Whisk spent hours watching the fireflies dance and twirl in the moonlight, their laughter blending with the soft music of the forest.

Another time, they encountered a mischievous squirrel named Nutty who challenged them to a game of acorn bowling. Nutty had collected acorns of all shapes and sizes, and he taught Sammy and Whisk how to roll them down a mossy hill, trying to knock over a line of pinecone pins. It was a rollicking game that left them all in fits of giggles.

The Whimsical Forest never ceased to amaze Sammy and Whisk, and each adventure deepened their friendship and the forest's magic. Word of their extraordinary journeys continued to spread throughout the village, and children from near and far began to visit the forest in search of their own whimsical adventures.

Sammy and Whisk, now the unofficial guardians of the Whimsical Forest, welcomed these young explorers with open arms. They shared their favorite spots, introduced them to the talking animals, and even taught them the secret songs that made the flowers bloom in a riot of colors.

As the years passed, Sammy grew from a young boy into a wise and caring young man, and Whisk's tree flourished with his love and the laughter of countless children. The bond between Sammy and Whisk remained unbreakable, and they continued to explore the Whimsical Forest together, discovering new wonders with each passing season.

In the cozy cottage at the edge of the lively village, Sammy and Whisk's story continued to be told. It showed that friendship is like magic, and the Whimsical Forest was full of amazing surprises. Many kids in the years to come would still go on adventures in the forest, inspired by Sammy and his special friend, Whisk. Their friendship was like a treasure that never got old.

The end.

Story 7

Lena and the Courageous Cavern

In a small cottage at the edge of a quaint village, there lived a young girl named Lena. Lena had a heart that was as big as the sky and a spirit filled with curiosity. But what she loved most was exploring the world around her.

One sunny morning, as Lena was taking a walk on the outskirts of the village, she noticed something unusual—a hidden pathway leading into the heart of the forest. The villagers had always spoken of the forest as a place of mystery and danger, but Lena's curiosity got the better of her.

Lena took a big breath and felt really brave. She walked onto a secret path and went further into the woods. The woods were thick with lots of animals and plants. Lena quickly knew that this place was very special.

While Lena kept going on her adventure, she heard a sweet, musical humming. She followed the sound until she came to a big open space.

There, she found a special tree. Its leaves sparkled like emeralds, and it danced to its own happy song. This was the Whimsical Tree, and it talked to Lena in a kind voice.

"Hello, brave friend," the tree said. "I can feel that you're really curious and love adventure. Would you like to go on a special journey that will help you be even braver and stronger?"

Lena, feeling very excited, said yes to the adventure. The Whimsical Tree told her she needed to go to the middle of the forest and find the Courageous Cavern. It was a place where stories said the bravest people had to pass a big bravery test.

Lena began her adventure with a map given by the Whimsical Tree. She walked through thick bushes, crossed bubbling streams, and climbed steep hills. While she journeyed, she met forest animals who shared stories about being brave.

One of them was a wise old owl named Oliver. He had once saved his friends during a really bad storm. Another was a friendly squirrel named Squeaks, who had overcome his fear of heights to help a bird's nest that had fallen down.

As Lena journeyed deeper into the forest, she felt her own courage growing. She remembered the tales of bravery she had heard and drew strength from them.

Lena came to the entrance of the Courageous Cavern. It looked really dark and spooky, and strange sounds came from inside. But Lena knew it was the biggest test of her bravery.

She bravely went inside the cave. It was like a twisty, dark maze with lots of shadows and echoes. As she went further, she faced her biggest fears – like being scared of the dark, not knowing what's ahead, and

being afraid of not doing well.

But Lena didn't give up. She remembered the stories of brave people and used their courage to help her. Every step made her less afraid and stronger.

At last, she reached the heart of the Courageous Cavern. There, she found a shining crystal. This crystal was full of bravery, and when Lena touched it, she felt a big rush of courage inside her.

With the crystal in hand, Lena retraced her steps and emerged from the cavern, her heart brimming with bravery. She returned to the Whimsical Tree and shared her tale of triumph.

The Whimsical Tree smiled proudly. "Lena, you were very brave," it said. "Remember, being brave doesn't mean you're never scared, but it means you can be strong even when you are. Keep this in your heart, and you'll be able to do amazing things."

42

Lena thanked the Whimsical Tree and went back to her village. She told everyone about her brave adventure, and it inspired them. They decided to face their own fears and find their courage.

In her little cottage on the edge of the village, Lena kept exploring the world around her. She knew that being brave wasn't just about going into the unknown; it was also about finding the strength inside yourself to overcome it.

As the seasons passed, Lena's reputation as the bravest girl in the village kept growing. She became a role model for the other kids, who admired her a lot. They looked to her for help and advice on how to be brave and face their own fears.

One fall day, Lena got a special invite from the Whimsical Tree. The message made her really happy. It said, "Dear Lena, your bravery inspired everyone and even the magical creatures of the forest. We invite you to a big party just for you in the Heart of the Forest."

Lena said yes to the invite and went on a new adventure with her pals, Oliver the owl and Squeaks the squirrel. While they journeyed, more forest creatures heard about Lena's bravery and wanted to come to the party too.

The journey to the Heart of the Forest was filled with laughter, songs, and stories. Lena's heart swelled with happiness as she realized the impact of her bravery on the world around her.

When they got to the Heart of the Forest, Lena saw something amazing. The magical creatures had made the place look super pretty with fireflies, bright flowers, and shiny leaves. It was a big party to celebrate bravery, and Lena was the special guest.

The Whimsical Tree talked again, saying, "Lena, going to the

Courageous Cavern was just the start of your adventures. You've shown us that bravery is not just something we have, but something we can give to others. Your courage brought us all together, and that's why we're celebrating you today."

While Lena enjoyed the party, she thought about how bravery wasn't just about facing her own fears but also about helping others do the same. She figured out that real bravery was like a bright light that could make even the darkest places better and bring everyone closer in happiness and togetherness.

Lena's adventures went on, and now she had not just her bravery but also the bravery she had encouraged in others. The Heart of the Forest turned into a spot for friendship and bravery, where magical creatures and people got together to celebrate the strength of being brave.

In the end, Lena had a really big heart, stayed super curious, and her bravery was a forever gift to the world. The Courageous Cavern didn't just test her bravery; it started a bravery fire that would shine for many, many years.

The end.

Story 8

Oliver and the Timless Tree

Once upon a time, in a cozy little house near a quiet village, there was a boy named Oliver. Oliver had a big heart like the ocean and loved to explore and ask questions. But what he really wanted to learn was how to be patient.

Oliver had heard tales of the Timeless Tree—a tree that was said to stand at the heart of a hidden forest, where time moved differently. It was said that those who visited the Timeless Tree would learn the invaluable lesson of patience.

With a map and a heart full of determination, Oliver set off on his journey to find the Timeless Tree. The forest was dense, and the path was filled with twists and turns. But Oliver was eager to learn the art of patience, and he pressed on.

As Oliver walked further into the forest, he saw a nice rabbit named Rosie. Rosie was happily eating some tasty clover. Rosie seemed very calm and didn't rush around like everyone else.

"Excuse me," Oliver said, "I'm on a quest to find the Timeless Tree to learn about patience. Can you offer any guidance?"

Rosie stopped eating, and her little whiskers moved as she thought for a moment. She said, "Learning to be patient is like learning from the world around you. Let's sit here for a while and watch the world together."

Oliver thought that was a great idea, so he sat down next to Rosie. Together, they looked at the birds flying in the trees, the leaves dancing in the wind, and the sunshine peeking through the leaves above them.

As they spent more time together, Oliver started to feel very peaceful. He understood that patience wasn't just about waiting for something, but also about enjoying what's happening right now. The gentle sound of leaves in the breeze sounded like a calming song, and the sunlight shining through the trees made the forest floor look like a magical dance of light and shadow.

Oliver felt wiser and more thankful for his time with Rosie. He said goodbye to her and continued his journey. The path led him to a meadow filled with colorful butterflies. They were like living rainbows, dancing and twirling in the air with so much beauty and grace.

Oliver walked up to the butterflies and asked, "I'm on a special adventure to find the Timeless Tree to learn about patience. Can you give me some advice?"

One of the butterflies, a stunning mix of blue and orange, gently landed on Oliver's hand. It said, "Patience is a lot like how we butterfly dance. It's about moving gracefully and enjoying every moment as it happens."

Oliver sat and watched the butterflies dance for a long time. He loved their pretty colors and the way they moved. He learned that patience meant enjoying the journey, not just waiting. The butterflies showed him that each moment is special, and when you put them all together, they make something beautiful.

Feeling thankful, Oliver said goodbye to the butterflies and went further into the forest. He found a stream where turtles were sunbathing.

"I'm on a journey to find the Timeless Tree and learn about patience," Oliver told the turtles. "Can you help me?"

The oldest turtle, a wise one with a fancy patterned shell, looked at Oliver. "Patience is like how we sunbathe," the turtle said. "It means going slow and enjoying every warm moment."

Oliver sat with the turtles by the stream. He felt the sun on his skin, making him happy. He learned that patience is about enjoying the simple things in life, not just waiting for hard times to pass. The sound of the babbling brook was like a soothing bedtime song, and the leaves above him made a gentle song.

Feeling wise, Oliver said thanks to the turtles and kept going. He walked deeper into the forest and found a babbling brook. The brook talked about the Timeless Tree, its branches touching the sky and its roots deep in the earth.

At last, Oliver reached the center of the secret forest. There, he found the Timeless Tree, a tall and magnificent tree. Its branches reached high into the sky, and its leaves whispered with ancient knowledge.

Oliver walked up to the tree and said, "I've come here to learn about patience. Can you teach me?"

The Timeless Tree whispered like the wind, and Oliver closed his eyes to listen. He felt time slow down, like moments lasting forever, and he learned what patience really meant. He felt like he was part of the forest, connected to the Earth's heartbeat and filled with wisdom from long ago.

When Oliver went back to his village, he told everyone what he'd learned. He said patience wasn't just waiting but enjoying the now, finding happiness in the journey, loving simple things, and knowing the wise side of being patient.

And so, in the charming cottage on the outskirts of the peaceful village, Oliver continued to explore the world around him, knowing that the art of patience was a treasure worth seeking and sharing. The people in the village saw how wise Oliver was, and they started to look at the world in a new way. They found happiness in the simple things, like watching butterflies, hearing leaves in the wind, and listening to the babbling streams. They made their village a place where time felt slow, and nature's wonders were celebrated.

Oliver's cottage became a special spot where people who wanted to learn patience would gather. Oliver's heart was as big as the ocean, and he always stayed curious and thankful for the beauty of the world. This is how the story of Oliver and the Timeless Tree began, reminding everyone that patience isn't just a lesson; it's a way of living in harmony with the changing world around us.

The end.

Story 9

Ava and the Secret of Happiness

Once upon a time, in a small, happy village, there was a young girl named Ava. Ava always felt warm and joyful inside. But she had a question in her mind: "How can I be even happier?"

One sunny morning, as Ava walked through a flowery field, she saw a special butterfly. This butterfly was different from any she'd seen before. Its wings sparkled with colors she couldn't even describe. It danced in the air, making her feel super happy.

Ava followed the butterfly, and it took her to a secret place in the meadow. Under a very old oak tree, she met a funny creature named Happy.

Happy was round and cheerful all the time. "Hello, Ava!" Happy said happily. "I'm the Happiness Keeper. Since you followed the butterfly, I guess you want to know the happiness secret."

Ava nodded with excitement. "Yes, I really do! What's the secret, Happy?"

50

Happy motioned for Ava to join it on a comfy mossy spot. "The secret to happiness isn't in stuff or places," Happy started. "It's in your heart and how you look at the world."

Ava paid close attention as Happy told stories about folks and creatures who found happiness in easy things like giggles with friends, watching the sun come up, and helping others.

"But," Ava thought, "what if there are tough times or sad moments in life? Can you still find happiness?"

Happy nodded, "For sure! Life has good times and bad times, but the trick is to find happiness even when things are tough. It's like having a light inside you that always shines."

With Happy's help, Ava started a journey to find happiness in everyday things. She loved her friends' laughter and the birds' songs. She thought the flowers' colors were amazing, and the wind felt gentle.

One day, while exploring the forest, Ava met Sammy, a friendly squirrel. Sammy had lost his acorns and was really sad.

Ava sat down beside Sammy and asked, "Why do you look so sad, Sammy?"

Sammy sighed. "I've lost my acorns for the winter, and I don't know where to find them."

Ava smiled, remembering Happy's lessons. "Let's search for your acorns together, Sammy. We'll make a game out of it!"

Sammy felt so hopeful as they started looking for acorns together. They laughed, sang songs, and told stories as they searched. When the sun was about to set, they found the last missing acorn.

Sammy felt really thankful and said, "Ava, you've made me super happy today!"

Ava saw that helping Sammy made her happy too. She learned that being kind and having friends could fill her heart with joy.

As she continued her journey, Ava met a grumpy old turtle named Timmy. Timmy complained about the slow pace of life and how everything took too long.

Ava remembered Happy's lessons once more. She sat down with Timmy and said, "Let's take a moment to enjoy the beauty of this meadow, Timmy. Sometimes, slowing down can help us find happiness."

Timmy wasn't sure at first, but he decided to give it a go. They saw the sun go down, and it made the meadow look warm and pretty. Timmy couldn't stop smiling.

"You were right, Ava," Timmy said. "This was a lovely moment. I feel happier now."

Ava learned that even in surprising places, you could find happiness by seeing things in a new way.

With her heart full of wisdom and joy, Ava went back to Happy in the hidden grove. She thanked Happy for the important lessons and told her own stories about finding happiness all around her.

Happy looked really proud. "Ava, you've figured out the happiness secret. It's not something you find like treasure; it's a gift you share. When you see the beauty in the world and are kind to others, you make not only yourself happy but also others."

So, in the cozy cottage on the edge of the happy village, Ava kept

exploring the world with a heart full of joy. She knew that happiness was a choice she could make every day.

Ava walked back to her cottage that evening, thinking about her amazing journey with Happy's help. She now knew that the happiness secret wasn't just in her heart but also in making others happy through kindness and positivity.

One evening, Ava decided to share her happiness secret with the villagers by inviting them to a special meeting in the meadow, where she and Happy would discuss it. The villagers, intrigued by Ava's contagious happiness, eagerly accepted her invitation.

As the sun went down, making the meadow glow with warm, golden light, Ava stood in front of the villagers with Happy by her side.

She began, "I have learned that the secret to happiness is not a distant treasure or a dream. It's a choice we make every day to find joy in the simplest of things and to share that joy with others."

Ava told the villagers about how she helped Sammy the squirrel and Timmy the turtle. She talked about how being kind had made her happy and brought joy to others.

Happy added, "Don't forget, happiness can shine even in tough times because it's a light inside you."

The villagers listened closely, and their faces showed they understood. Ava's words meant a lot to them. They realized that they didn't have to chase happiness all the time. Instead, they could grow it inside themselves and share it with everyone in their village.

Ava's smart thinking and Happy's happiness made the villagers very happy. They decided to make a happiness club. They met often to tell stories about being happy, kind, and thankful, and they made everyone in the village happy too.

The village, which was already happy, became even more lively. The villagers saw the world in a new way. They found happiness in pretty flowers, kids laughing, and helping their neighbors.

Ava, always happy in her heart, kept showing the village that they could choose to be happy every day.

In the cozy cottage on the edge of the happy village, Ava's search for happiness had not just made her life better but also made the whole village better. It showed that happiness was a special gift that could be found and shared by people with open hearts.

The end.

Story 10

Lily and the Art of Communication

Once upon a time, in a little house by the edge of a beautiful village, there was a young girl named Lily. Lily had a heart that was as warm as the sun, and she loved to explore and learn new things. But most of all, she wanted to know how to talk to others in the best way.

One sunny morning, Lily went into the nearby forest. As she walked among the trees, she noticed something very special. The trees were not just standing still; they were talking to each other! Their leaves were making soft sounds, like a secret song.

Lily was so curious that she went closer to the trees. She reached out and gently touched the bark of one tree. To her surprise, the tree answered with a gentle rustling sound, as if it wanted to say something.

"Can you teach me how to talk like you do?" Lily asked the tree, her eyes wide with wonder.

The tree rustled again, and it felt like it was saying, "Yes, we can help you learn about communication."

Lily was filled with excitement, for she knew this was the start of a wonderful adventure in the world of talking to others. She was about to learn some amazing secrets from the whispering trees!

The tree that Lily touched, an old oak named Oliver, made a friendly sound. "Communication isn't just about words. It's about making a special connection by understanding, caring, and showing things without speaking."

Oliver, the smart old oak, told Lily that each tree in the grove had a special job in the forest. Some trees gave homes to birds, others gave shade to animals when it got hot, and a few even shared their yummy fruits with hungry creatures. Lily found these stories super interesting. She realized that good communication was about more than just talking. It meant doing things, showing with your actions, and, most importantly, understanding how others felt.

With these tree lessons in her heart, Lily went back to her village. She was excited to practice what she had learned about talking to others. She started by really listening to her friends and family. She wanted to truly understand what they needed and how they felt.

As Lily learned, there's more to communication than just words. It's about showing you care, and that can make a big difference in how you connect with others.

When her younger brother, Ethan, had a tough day at school, Lily sat with him and listened patiently to his worries. She offered a comforting hug and shared her own experiences to show him that he was not alone.

As Lily continued to hone her communication skills, she found

herself forming deeper connections with those around her. She discovered that the true power of communication was not just in speaking but in understanding and empathy.

One day, while exploring the forest, Lily met a friendly rabbit named Rosie. Rosie had lost her way and was feeling terribly anxious.

Lily knelt down beside Rosie and asked, "Why do you look so worried, Rosie?"

Rosie, a little rabbit, was feeling very scared. She spoke with a shaky voice, telling Lily that she had gone too far from her cozy burrow and didn't know how to get back.

Lily, always kind and caring, smiled softly and said, "It's okay, Rosie. I'll help you find your way home."

Lily was patient and full of kindness. She led Rosie back to her burrow, step by step, making sure Rosie felt safe and not alone. Lily stayed with Rosie until she was sure Rosie was comfortable before continuing her own adventure.

Lily knew that helping others and being there for friends was just as important as learning to communicate. It was all part of being a good friend and a kind person.

As Lily walked away, she felt something warm inside her heart. Helping Rosie had made her really happy. Lily had learned that being kind and talking to others in a nice way made her heart feel full of joy.

As the weeks passed, more and more people in the village knew that Lily was a kind and caring friend. They came to her when they needed help or advice because they knew she would listen and understand them.

So, in her little house at the edge of the pretty village, Lily kept on exploring the world. She talked to people with love and care, knowing that it helped them feel better. And she kept visiting her special grove of talking trees. Those trees taught her about nature and how to talk in a special way that made the world better.

Lily's kindness made everyone in the village want to be better at talking and understanding each other. They even planted their own talking trees in their gardens, hoping to learn more.

One summer, Lily threw a big picnic in the forest for the whole village. It was a day of fun, with singing, laughing, and stories from the talking trees. Everyone felt closer to nature, thanks to Lily's lessons. They promised to take care of the forest for a long, long time.

As time went by, Lily grew up and became a smart and caring woman. She never stopped spreading the message of kindness and good talking wherever she went. Her heart, once curious, now had lots of love for the world and everyone in it.

And so, in her cozy little house by the pretty village, Lily's story lived on. It became a favorite story for kids at bedtime. It reminded them to be kind, to understand each other, and to love the beautiful world around them.

The end.

Story 11

Lep and the Leap of Courage

A long time ago, in a small house near a busy village, there lived a young boy named Leo. Everyone in the village admired Leo because he was very courageous and never gave up, no matter what. But Leo had a special dream hidden in his heart. He wished to discover how to deal with tough challenges and learn from them.

Once upon a bright and sunny morning, Leo felt a burst of adventure bubbling inside him. He wanted to go on a big adventure in the village square! Leo's eyes sparkled with curiosity as he saw a bunch of kids gathered around something very interesting.

What do you think they were looking at? It was a special sign! This sign told everyone about a super exciting challenge. The whole village was buzzing with excitement because of it! What was the challenge, you ask? Well, it was an incredible, gigantic jump over a big, fast river that flowed gently through their peaceful village.

The kids were talking and laughing, and Leo wanted to join them.

But before he could take part in the challenge, he had to practice and learn how to jump really, really far.

Leo felt a mixture of feelings - he was both excited and scared. He had always been curious about what lay on the other side of the river, but the thought of making such a big jump seemed almost impossible. The river was powerful and deep, and nobody in the village had ever managed to cross it before.

Leo's adventurous heart led him to step closer to the group. With curiosity in his eyes, he asked the kids, "How can I prepare for the jump?"

Mia, a courageous girl who had attempted the jump in the past, stepped forward with a kind smile. "Leo," she said gently, "it's not only about having physical strength. It's about having faith in yourself and being brave enough to confront your fears."

Mia went on to tell Leo something really important. She said, "Leo, you know, the hardest part of this challenge isn't the river itself; it's the doubts and fears that can hold you back." Mia had some amazing stories to share with Leo about people who were just like him, feeling a bit scared but still taking a leap into the unknown.

With a twinkle in her eye, Mia explained, "You see, Leo, that river might look big and a little scary, but it's the worries in our minds that make it seem even scarier. The truly brave folks who faced their fears found incredible surprises and exciting adventures waiting for them on the other side. It's just like opening a treasure chest filled with new, wonderful experiences!"

With Mia's warm and encouraging words safely tucked in his heart, Leo began his training adventure. Day after day, he spent hours practicing his jumps, growing stronger with each leap. He

also learned the secret of keeping his fears in check. But the most precious lesson he discovered was the power of believing in himself.

Leo understood that believing in himself meant he could achieve amazing things. It was like having a magical superpower that made him feel capable of taking on any challenge that came his way.

The big day for the great leap had finally come, and everyone in the village gathered by the riverbank, filled with excitement. Leo stood right at the edge, his heart beating fast with a mix of both fear and determination. The river in front of him was making a loud sound, with its swirling waters stretching out wide. It was a moment filled with lots of feelings, and Leo was ready to take a deep breath and jump into the unknown.

Leo stepped back, taking a deep breath. He closed his eyes briefly and imagined himself succeeding. Then, with all the bravery and strength he had, he jumped into the air. It felt like time was going slower as he felt the wind blowing around him. For a little while, his heart raced as he hung in the air. And then, with a big splash, he landed safely on the other side, feeling triumphant and happy.

The village burst into joyful cheers, and Leo's heart grew as big as a hot air balloon with pride. He had met his fears head-on and accepted the challenge with open arms. And in this daring act, he had found something really important: a special secret. It was like a treasure hidden in a storybook.

Leo learned that sometimes, the most wonderful things in life are waiting for us on the far side of fear. Just like finding a hidden path in the woods that leads to a magical garden filled with colorful flowers and friendly butterflies. Leo had discovered that when you're brave and give your best, the world can be full of amazing surprises, just like the ones in the most enchanting fairy tales.

With his fresh confidence, Leo ventured further into the world beyond the river. There, he uncovered secret treasures hidden in the most unexpected places, made friends who laughed and played with him, and encountered the most incredible adventures that felt like stories from a magical book. Leo realized that challenges were not big scary walls but were like doors leading to exciting discoveries.

Back in his cozy cottage at the edge of the bustling village, Leo kept exploring the world with his heart filled with courage. He understood that every challenge that crossed his path was an invitation to reach for the stars. And as the sun dipped below the horizon, painting the village in warm, golden colors, Leo's spirit glowed brightly, like a guiding star, inspiring everyone who knew him to be brave and never give up on their dreams.

The end.

Story 12

The Friendshop Bridge

Once upon a time, in a tiny, cheerful village nestled right next to a calm and friendly river, there was a bunch of kids. These kids were as different from each other as the colors in a beautiful rainbow. They were famous in their village for two special things. They loved going on exciting adventures, and they really wanted to be friends with everyone they met.

One sunny day, when the children were playing near the river's edge, they saw something super interesting. It was something they'd never seen before—a huge, shimmering river that seemed to go on forever. It was called the River of Friendship, a magical waterway that was believed to connect the hearts of friends no matter how far apart they were.

The kids were so excited, and they couldn't stop themselves from wondering about this amazing river. They wondered how it worked and how they could use it to make new friends. And among these kids was Mia, a girl who was really clever and loved figuring out puzzles.

Mia paused for a moment, her eyes sparkling with inspiration. She smiled and said, "I've got a fantastic idea! What if we create something special—a Friendship Bridge? With it, we can reach out to friends who are really far away!"

The other children were overjoyed with Mia's idea. They all agreed enthusiastically and got to work right away. They gathered all sorts of materials and started sketching their grand design. They envisioned a bridge that would be wide enough for all of them to walk together, and they dreamed of decorating it with handrails covered in colorful flags from different countries around the world.

With hearts full of determination and hands full of teamwork, the children began building the Friendship Bridge. It stretched across the shimmering River of Friendship, connecting their village to faraway lands. And as the bridge took shape, they proudly added those colorful flags to the handrails. When the wind blew, the flags danced merrily, sending a message of unity and friendship to all who saw them.

Every day, the children would rush to the Friendship Bridge, their hearts bursting with excitement, eager to meet new friends. They'd line up along the bridge, waving and shouting joyful hellos across the river, their voices filled with the hope of hearing the warm replies of their faraway buddies.

Then, one magical day, a boy named Kavi from a village miles away appeared on the other side of the Friendship Bridge. His eyes sparkled with curiosity as he saw the colorful flags and heard the laughter echoing from the bridge.

The children didn't waste a second; they welcomed Kavi with the biggest smiles and open arms, inviting him to step onto the

Friendship Bridge and be part of their games and adventures. And the moment Kavi set foot on that special bridge, something truly magical happened. He felt like he belonged right there with them, and a warm, fuzzy feeling of friendship wrapped around him like a cozy blanket, making him happier than he'd ever been before.

"I've traveled to many places," Kavi said with a smile, "but I've never met friends as amazing as all of you."

As the day went on, the children and Kavi became fast friends. They shared stories about their lives, played games that made them laugh until their tummies hurt, and even exchanged little gifts to show their newfound friendship. It was amazing to see that, even though they spoke different languages and had different customs, they had so many things in common and shared the same big dreams for a world filled with happiness and friendship.

As the golden sun dipped below the horizon, Kavi beamed and said, "I've made friends I'll cherish forever. I promise I'll come back to the Friendship Bridge soon."

With those words, Kavi returned to his village, carrying with him the memories of the children and the happiness of their newfound friendships.

News of the Friendship Bridge and the wonderful connections it made spread like wildfire. Children from nearby villages and even far lands came to visit. The bridge became a place where friendships bloomed and grew stronger, reminding everyone that no matter where you come from, friendship knows no bounds.

One sunny day, a bunch of kids from a village very far away came to visit the Friendship Bridge. Right in the middle of the group was Zara, a girl who absolutely adored making music. She had with her a colorful drum that looked like a rainbow, and she started to play a joyful tune.

The children at the Friendship Bridge couldn't help but dance and giggle to the joyful music. The drum's happy beat and the sounds of their friendship floated in the air along the River of Friendship, making a beautiful melody that seemed to go on forever.

Zara and the new friends from the faraway village had a day full of music and laughter. They discovered something amazing: music was like a secret code that everyone could understand, no matter where they were from. It could bring people together like nothing else.

As the sun began to set, Zara promised, "I'll come back with even more friends and more music. The Friendship Bridge is truly a magical place."

And magical it was indeed! The Friendship Bridge kept on doing its wonderful work as a symbol of togetherness and friendship. Kids from all corners of the world crossed it, making friends that didn't care about borders or differences.

And so, in that small, lively village next to the gentle river, the children learned that friendships could sprout up in the most unexpected spots. They realized that the Friendship Bridge wasn't just a bridge made of bricks and wood; it was a bridge of the heart, connecting people from all walks of life, and reminding everyone that friendship knows no boundaries.

The end.

Story 13

The Magical Ice Cream Chart

Once upon a time, in the cozy little town of Harmonyville, there was a young girl named Mia. Everyone in town loved Mia because she always had a warm heart and a smile that made everyone feel happy. But Mia had a special challenge she wanted to conquer - it was called "self-control."

You see, Mia had a super-duper love for ice cream. Whenever she heard the ice cream truck's jingly music, her heart would dance with joy, and she couldn't resist the sight of colorful ice cream scoops piled high on a crunchy cone. But here's the thing - Mia had a tiny problem. She often found it really hard to stop at just one scoop.

One sunny afternoon, while Mia was playing in the park with her friends, she heard that familiar ice cream truck jingle. Her friends, all excited, rushed over to get their ice cream. Mia stopped for a moment, feeling a bit worried because she knew her self-control would be tested.

But Mia wasn't one to back down from a challenge. With a determined look on her face, she decided to give it her best shot and show herself that she could do it. She took a deep breath, walked over to the ice cream truck, and made her choice. What do you think Mia did next? Let's find out!

Mia took a deep breath and bravely stood in line with her friends. She decided that today would be the day she showed self-control and only get one scoop of ice cream. As she got closer to the ice cream cart, her eyes grew wide with wonder at all the different flavors and toppings.

With a friendly smile, Mr. Whipple, the ice cream vendor, asked, "What can I get you, dear?"

Mia replied with a big smile, "I'll have a single scoop of chocolate chip, please."

As Mr. Whipple handed Mia her ice cream, she felt a sense of achievement wash over her. She had proven to herself that she could exercise self-control and resist the temptation to get more.

Mia happily rejoined her friends on the park benches, taking small, delightful bites of her ice cream. It was scrumptious, and she couldn't help but feel proud of herself for sticking to her decision.

As the days turned into weeks, Mia kept practicing self-control every time the ice cream truck visited Harmonyville. She would pick her favorite flavor and enjoy every spoonful, resisting the urge to go back for seconds. Mia had learned that with determination and a warm heart, she could conquer any challenge, even the most delicious ones!

One sunny afternoon, something truly magical happened. Mia found herself at the end of the line at the ice cream truck, and Mr. Whipple had a fantastic surprise waiting for her. He said, "Mia, today

you've shown incredible self-control. As a special treat, I'm going to give you a token for the Magical Ice Cream Cart."

Mia's eyes grew as big as saucers with excitement. She had heard whispers and rumors about the Magical Ice Cream Cart, a mysterious cart that only appeared to those who had shown extraordinary self-control.

With a flourish, Mr. Whipple handed Mia a gleaming, shimmering token, and right before her eyes, the cart materialized. It was unlike any ice cream cart she had ever seen, adorned with golden swirls and sparkling lights.

Inside the cart, the ice cream vendor was none other than the Ice Cream Fairy, a mystical figure known for granting special ice cream wishes to those who had earned them through self-control.

The Ice Cream Fairy beamed at Mia and asked, "What is your ice cream wish today, dear child?"

Mia thought for a moment, her heart filled with kindness and warmth. Then she said, "I wish for a special ice cream that will make everyone in Harmonyville happy."

With a magical twinkle in her eye, the Ice Cream Fairy waved her wand, and from the cart emerged an ice cream like no other. It sparkled with joy and shimmered with happiness. As Mia took a bite, she could feel the love and laughter of the entire town filling her heart.

From that day on, Mia's special ice cream became the town's favorite treat. Whenever anyone needed a little pick-me-up, they would head to the Magical Ice Cream Cart, and Mia's wish would spread happiness all around Harmonyville.

And so, Mia learned that sometimes, the sweetest rewards come to those who show self-control and think of others. In Harmonyville, thanks to Mia's wish, smiles and laughter were as plentiful as ice cream on a sunny day.

The Ice Cream Fairy gave a nod, and with a wave of her magical wand, she created an ice cream cone like no other. It had rainbow-colored scoops and toppings that sparkled like stars in the night sky. When Mia took her very first bite, a burst of pure happiness swept over her.

With every scoop of the magical ice cream, Mia's joy multiplied. She couldn't keep this wonderful delight to herself, so she shared it with her friends and all the other children playing in the park. As they tasted the magical treat, their faces lit up with smiles, and the park was filled with the sound of joyful laughter.

News of this extraordinary ice cream spread like wildfire throughout Harmonyville. People from all corners of the town gathered in the park, eager to taste the happiness-inducing flavors for themselves. Mia's act of self-control had brought happiness to everyone in the town.

As the sun slowly set on that unforgettable day, Mia realized something important. Self-control wasn't just about saying "no" to tempting things; it was also about making choices that could bring happiness and kindness to others.

Mia continued to visit the Magical Ice Cream Cart whenever it appeared, sharing its happiness-inducing treats with her friends and neighbors. She had discovered that sometimes, the sweetest rewards came to those who exercised self-control and shared their joy with others.

And so, in the cozy little town of Harmonyville, everyone learned that self-control wasn't only about resisting temptations; it was about making choices that brought happiness, kindness, and magical moments into their lives. The town became a place filled not only with delicious ice cream but also with the sweet warmth of generosity and friendship.

The end.

Story 14

Adventure with Andy the Adaptable Ant

Once upon a time, in a busy anthill nestled deep within a lush meadow, lived a little ant named Andy. Andy was quite famous among all the ants in the anthill. Why, you ask? Well, it's because Andy was always full of questions and loved to explore new things. He was a little ant with a big heart for learning and growing.

Andy's favorite lesson in life was all about change and discovering new things. He believed that it was important to adapt and learn, just like how he had to navigate through the twists and turns of the anthill tunnels. Andy knew that when you're open to new experiences and ideas, life becomes a thrilling adventure.

And so, in the heart of the bustling anthill, Andy the curious ant embarked on exciting journeys of learning and change, inspiring all his ant friends to do the same.

You see, the ant colony was a place where things were always changing. Sometimes, the weather was super-hot, and other times, it rained a lot. The places where they found food would appear and disappear, and the tunnels they made were always moving. Andy knew that to do well in this ever-changing world, he had to learn how to change and adjust.

One bright and sunny morning, as Andy joined his ant buddies in their quest to gather food, something quite unusual occurred. Suddenly, the earth beneath their tiny feet rumbled, and a loud rumbling noise echoed through the air. Oh no! It was a big rainstorm heading their way!

Most of the ants got scared and ran back to their cozy anthill to stay safe from the rain. But not Andy! He thought this was a chance to do something amazing. Andy was really smart and good at coming up with ideas. He gathered some of his ant pals and talked to them about a special plan.

They decided to collect big leaves and put them together like a roof. It was a super clever idea! When they were done, they had a huge leafy roof over their heads. It kept them dry and snug while the rain poured down all around.

When the storm was over, Andy felt so happy and proud of what they did. He showed everyone that he could face new challenges and come up with smart solutions. Andy turned a big problem into a fun adventure, and it worked out great!

News of Andy's cleverness quickly spread throughout the anthill, and soon, everyone started calling him "Andy the Adaptable Ant." Other ants began seeking out his help whenever they faced problems, and Andy was always there, ready to lend a hand and share his incredible problem-solving skills. Together, they learned that when they faced challenges with an open heart and a

willingness to adapt, they could turn any problem into an opportunity for growth and discovery.

One day, something really big happened to the ant colony. A huge

machine called a bulldozer, which was driven by humans, was getting closer to their meadow. The bulldozer looked like it would destroy their anthill and everything they loved.

All the ants got very worried and didn't know what to do. But then, Andy stepped up and said, "We have to change and deal with this new problem. We can't stop the bulldozer, but we can figure out how to stay safe."

With Andy leading the way, the ants worked really hard to move their whole ant home to a different meadow, far away from where the bulldozer was going. It was a really big job that needed them to change and work together, but they did it!

While the bulldozer knocked down their old anthill, the ants watched from their new home in the meadow. They learned that being able to change and work together didn't just help them survive; it helped them do even better when things around them changed.

In their new meadow, the ants found lots and lots of food and things they needed, things they didn't even know were there before. They made their colony even stronger and tougher, so they could deal with any problem that came along.

Time passed, and the meadow became their happy home. Andy, the ant who could change and learn, got older but smarter. He knew that being adaptable wasn't just about handling big problems; it was also about changing to meet the needs of the colony when things were different.

One sunny morning, Andy gathered all the young ants in the bustling anthill and spoke with a cheerful smile, "Hey, my dear ant pals, I'm about to embark on exciting new journeys, but I want you to always remember the valuable lesson I've shared with you about the magic of change. When things become different, don't fret or worry; instead, embrace it and use your wisdom to make our home even more wonderful."

Filled with gratitude and warmth in their little ant hearts, the ants bid farewell to Andy, the wise ant who had imparted the most important lesson of all: the power of adaptation. As he set off on his grand adventures, they knew that his ability to adapt would guide him well on his exciting path.

So, deep within their busy anthill nestled in the vibrant meadow, the ants continued to discover just how significant it was to be open to change. They soon realized that change wasn't something to be afraid of; instead, it brought marvelous opportunities to learn, to grow, and to make their future even more dazzling.

The end.

Story 15

The Great Dragon Boat Race

In a beautiful village next to a calm river, there lived four friends: Tom the tortoise, Lily the rabbit, Benny the bear, and Maya the monkey. They were still celebrating their amazing victory in the Great Dragon Boat Race. The whole village was full of happiness, and everyone kept talking about how the friends had won because they worked so well together.

Word of their big win traveled to nearby villages, and soon, they got special invitations to come and visit. These villages wanted to hear all about the friends' teamwork and how they became champions. Tom, Lily, Benny, and Maya loved new adventures, so they decided to go on a journey to tell everyone about the importance of working together and being good friends.

Their first stop was Meadowville, the village next door. The people there were super excited to see them. Tom, Lily, Benny, and Maya had an amazing story to share with the villagers. It was a tale of how they became champions through teamwork and helping each other. They had a very important lesson to pass on: when you work together and lend a hand to your friends, you can conquer any challenge that comes your way.

The people of Meadowville were so inspired by theirs' story that they decided to do something truly incredible. They dreamed of having their very own dragon boat race! And you won't believe it – Tom, Lily, Benny, and Maya were thrilled to help make this dream come true.

These four friends became like coaches for the dragon boat race. They put in lots of hard work for many weeks, teaching the folks in Meadowville how to paddle together perfectly and why teamwork was the secret ingredient to success. As the big day drew nearer, the excitement in Meadowville grew and grew. Everyone couldn't wait to see if they could be as successful as our wonderful friends.

At last, the big race day had come! So many folks, from close by and from really far away, came to see the fun. Imagine this: teams were all lined up, each with their own special dragon boat. These boats were super colorful and sparkled like magic in the bright sunshine.

Tom, Lily, Benny, and Maya, had big smiles on their faces. They felt super proud because they had been helping and teaching the teams for a long time. The teams were all set and super ready to begin the race. This day was packed with excitement and joy!

Once the race started, the teams in Meadowville showed off their incredible teamwork, all thanks to the great training and advice from Tom, Lily, Benny, and Maya. The feeling of togetherness filled the air, and the dragon boats moved gracefully over the water, just like our friends' boats had done when they won.

The competition was super tough, but the lessons about working together and never giving up were still fresh in everyone's minds. The Meadowville teams, inspired by our friends' story, put in all their effort. They paddled with all their hearts and matched their moves perfectly, like a well-trained orchestra playing beautiful music.

As they got nearer to the finish line, the crowd grew very, very excited. The race was so close, with a bunch of teams nearly in the same place. But in the end, one special team managed to move ahead and cross the finish line with their paddles held high in the air. They became the champions!

The cheers from the crowd were incredibly loud, and the Meadowville team was announced as the big winners. This proved just how incredible teamwork could be and how much our friends' story had inspired everyone. The cheers sounded like a gigantic party, and it felt like the entire world was joining in on the celebration.

Tom, Lily, Benny, and Maya felt so, so happy and proud. They realized that they hadn't just won their own race, but they had also inspired a whole other group of people to come together and do great things by working together. They understood that their journey was about more than just winning – it was about spreading the message of teamwork and friendship to lots of places.

So, the friends didn't give up. They kept on going with their adventure, visiting more villages and towns. Wherever they went, they told their story. People started calling them the "Teamwork Ambassadors," which was a super cool name, like having a superhero title! And you know what? Their exciting adventures were written in books that kids from all over the land read eagerly. They were making a really, really big difference and teaching everyone about the magic of working together and being great friends.

But guess what? The story didn't stop there! In villages near and far, people began to understand the importance of teamwork, just like our friends had taught them. They realized that when they joined their strengths and celebrated their differences, they could achieve awesome things and overcome any challenge that came their way.

In the end, what Tom the tortoise, Lily the rabbit, Benny the bear, and Maya the monkey accomplished was not just winning a dragon boat race. It was leaving behind a special gift – a legacy of togetherness and the everlasting power of teamwork. So, my dear kids, always remember that when you work together with your friends, support each other, and embrace your uniqueness, you can do incredible things, just like our amazing friends did!

The end.

Story 16

The Magic Apple tree

Once upon a time, in a charming village surrounded by big green hills and beautiful gardens bursting with colors, there were some very special friends who knew the secret of real magic – sharing! These pals included Emma the elephant, Sammy the squirrel, Mia the rabbit, and Leo the lion. Everybody in the village admired them because they were always happy to share with others.

One bright morning, when the sun was shining high in the sky, our friendly bunch gathered in their favorite meadow. As they chatted and giggled, something amazing caught their eye! It was a tree like no other tree they'd ever seen. Its leaves were as shiny as a rainbow, and its branches drooped low with the most extraordinary apples anyone had ever laid eyes on!

Sammy the squirrel, with his curious little eyes, couldn't help but wonder aloud, "What kind of tree is this?" His eyes sparkled with amazement.

Mia the rabbit bravely hopped over to the tree and picked one of those incredible apples. As she nibbled on it, she couldn't help but shout, "Oh my, this apple is the sweetest and juiciest I've ever tasted!"

Now, Leo the lion, famous for his bravery, decided to show just how brave he was. He began to climb the tree with confidence, his strong paws gripping the branches easily. Up, up, up he went, reaching the highest branches without a hint of fear. Leo gathered a bunch of those magical apples in his mighty arms, making the tree rustle with delight.

While enjoying the delicious apples, the friends soon realized that there were plenty to go around for everyone in the village. Emma the elephant had a bright idea. She said, "Why don't we invite everyone in the village to join us here in the meadow? We can share these magical apples with them. That way, everyone can feel their wonderful magic."

The idea made everyone's hearts flutter with excitement, and they got to work right away. Leo the lion let out a mighty roar that could be heard all over the village, beckoning the villagers to come to the meadow. It wasn't long before families and friends from every nook and cranny of the village gathered beneath the enchanting apple tree.

The friends started handing out the apples, making sure that each villager got one. As the villagers took a bite, their faces lit up with sheer joy. They couldn't believe the extraordinary flavor and the happiness that seemed to burst inside them like fireworks.

The friends had a wonderful secret to share. They explained that the magic apple tree was no ordinary tree; it had a very special power. You see, it could make people feel incredibly happy and satisfied. But, there was a little trick to it: the tree's magic worked best when people shared the apples with others.

As the days went by, the village transformed into a place filled with happiness and togetherness. People began to share these magical apples with their neighbors, and even strangers became fast friends as they passed apples to one another. The feeling of being together and the joy it brought were stronger than ever before.

News of this magic apple tree traveled far and wide, reaching neighboring towns and villages. Curious visitors came from all around to see this amazing tree for themselves. They too got to experience the tree's magic, and they couldn't help but carry the wonderful message of sharing and happiness back to their own homes. It was a ripple of joy that spread far and wide, all thanks to the magical tree and the friends who understood the power of sharing.

But as more and more people came to visit the magical tree, the friends began to notice something important. The tree's branches were starting to droop, weighed down by the abundance of apples it bore.

This was a clear sign that the tree needed some tender loving care.

So, the friends decided to gather all the villagers for a special meeting to talk about the tree's well-being. They explained that if everyone wanted to keep enjoying the magical apples, they needed to join together in looking after the tree and making sure it stayed healthy.

The villagers loved this idea, and they all agreed to pitch in. They set up a schedule to take turns caring for the tree. Every family in the village took on the responsibility of watering, pruning, and giving the tree lots of love and attention so it could keep producing its magical fruit. It was a way for everyone to show their gratitude to the tree for all the happiness it had brought into their lives.

With the hard work and love from the villagers, the magic apple tree not only survived but thrived. Its branches grew even stronger, and its leaves sparkled with an even more enchanting shimmer. The villagers did more than just share the apples; they also shared the important job of taking care of the tree.

Years rolled by, and the village remained a place filled with happiness and togetherness. The magic apple tree became a symbol of the village, a constant reminder to everyone about how vital it was to share, stay united, and care for one another.

So, in this charming village tucked away amidst rolling hills and gardens bursting with colors, people learned a truly magical lesson about sharing. They discovered that by not only sharing their treasures but also sharing their responsibilities, they could create a world where happiness and togetherness thrived, just like the magic apple tree in their midst.

The end.

Story 17

The Tale of Lucy the Listening Owl

Long, long ago, in a forest filled with magic, there was a young owl named Lucy. She made her cozy home under the giant, old trees. Lucy was famous among all the animals in the woods because she had the biggest, most attentive ears anyone had ever seen. But you know what Lucy loved the most? It was the wonderful lesson of listening.

Every day, Lucy would sit on her favorite branch and listen to the forest. She heard the rustling of leaves as the wind whispered secrets, the pitter-patter of raindrops on the leaves, and the chirping of birds sharing their stories. Lucy loved to close her eyes and let the sounds of the forest fill her heart.

She listened so well that she could tell when a squirrel had lost its acorns or when a rabbit needed a friend. Lucy even knew when the trees were happy and when they were sad. She would hoot softly to comfort them when they felt down.

Lucy's gift of listening didn't just make her famous; it made her a true friend to all the creatures in the magical forest. They knew they could always count on Lucy to lend an ear and a kind heart. And so, in the heart of the enchanted woods, Lucy lived happily, sharing the beautiful lesson of listening with everyone she met.

You see, the forest was not just any forest; it was a place brimming with stories waiting to be heard. The leaves rustled like storytellers, sharing secrets of the wind's far-off adventures. The babbling brooks gurgled with tales of the creatures they had encountered on their winding journeys, and the animals themselves had stories to tell. Lucy understood that by listening, she could uncover the boundless beauty and wisdom hidden within the forest's heart.

One bright and sun-dappled morning, as Lucy perched on her favorite branch, she heard a soft, melodic voice. It was a little bird named Benny, perched on a nearby branch, singing a sweet and enchanting song. Lucy closed her eyes and listened intently, savoring every note, letting the music wash over her like a gentle rain.

When Benny finished his song, he noticed Lucy and asked, "Did you like my song, Lucy?"

Lucy opened her eyes and nodded with a warm smile. "Benny, your song was more than beautiful; it filled my heart with joy and painted the forest with colors of happiness. Thank you for sharing it."

Benny blushed with delight and said, "I sing my songs to share happiness with others. Knowing that you enjoyed it makes me very, very happy."

From that day on, Lucy became known as "Lucy the Listening Owl" because she spent her days not only listening to the stories and songs of the forest but also to the hearts of its inhabitants. She listened to the wise old trees as they whispered their centuries of growth, to the gurgling brooks as they told of their journeys from the lofty mountains, and to the animals as they shared their tales of adventure and discovery.

But Lucy didn't stop at listening to the forest's stories; she also listened to the creatures who called it home. She listened when the squirrels had worries to share, when the rabbits had dreams to express, and when the deer needed comforting words.

One day, as Lucy was perched near a sparkling pond, she heard a tiny voice calling for help. It was Lilly, a young frog who had slipped into the water and was struggling to stay afloat. Lucy immediately swooped down and rescued Lilly from the pond.

Lilly, shivering and frightened, thanked Lucy with tears in her eyes. Lucy comforted her and listened as Lilly explained that she had been trying to catch a glimpse of the colorful fish that lived in the pond.

Lucy said, "Lilly, I'm glad I was here to listen to your call for help. But remember, sometimes it's important to listen to the advice of others, especially when it comes to safety."

Lilly nodded in agreement, grateful for the lesson she had learned. From that day on, she not only listened to her own curiosity but also to the wisdom of those around her.

As the seasons changed, Lucy's reputation as the Listening Owl grew far and wide. Creatures from distant forests would visit the magical woodland to share their stories with her. They knew that Lucy would listen with an open heart, and that their tales would be cherished like the most precious of treasures.

One enchanting evening, Lucy heard a gentle whisper in the wind. It was the ancient oak tree, the oldest and wisest in the forest. The tree shared a story of its long and majestic life, from a tiny acorn to a towering giant. Lucy listened with reverence, absorbing the wisdom of the ages.

With the knowledge she had gained from the ancient oak, Lucy began to teach the young creatures of the forest the importance of listening, not only to the stories of nature but also to the voices of others. She explained that through listening, they could understand, empathize, and learn from one another.

The young creatures embraced Lucy's teachings, and the forest became a place of deeper understanding and unity. They discovered that by truly listening to one another, they could build stronger bonds and face challenges together.

And so, in the magical forest beneath the towering, ancient trees, the creatures learned the profound lesson of listening. They discovered that by listening with open hearts and minds, they could uncover the beauty and wisdom of the world around them and create a place of everlasting harmony, empathy, and understanding. In this magical forest, the art of listening became a gift that would be passed down through generations, ensuring that the heartwarming tales and the wisdom of the woodland would endure for all time.

The end.

Story 18

Sammy and the Personal Space Lesson

Once upon a time, in a big, busy forest where animals of all shapes and sizes lived, there was a young squirrel named Sammy. Sammy was known for two things: he had lots and lots of energy, and he was very friendly. But what he cared about most was something really important - learning how to give others their own space.

In the enchanted forest, there was always something thrilling happening! Just like you and me, animals had their own treasured places. Now, let me tell you about Sammy, our inquisitive friend. Sammy was always up for a new adventure, and he had a question bubbling in his furry little heart. He wondered why these special spots meant so much to his woodland pals. And so, with a twinkle in his eye and a bounce in his step, Sammy set off on a delightful adventure to uncover the enchanting secrets of the forest!

One bright and cheerful morning, Sammy couldn't contain his excitement as he hopped from tree to tree. He couldn't wait to greet his friends, for he adored spending time with them, chatting, playing games, and sharing stories about their amazing adventures. But, oh dear, sometimes his boundless enthusiasm made him get just a tad too close for comfort.

One of his best friends, Ruby the rabbit, really liked having her own space. She loved her cozy burrow and felt worried when someone came in without asking. One day, Sammy jumped into her burrow without thinking, and Ruby said kindly but firmly, "Sammy, I really like being your friend, but please let me have my own space. My burrow is where I feel safe and relaxed."

Sammy blinked his big, round eyes and realized he had made a mistake. He felt bad for intruding on Ruby's space. He said, "I'm really sorry, Ruby. I didn't mean to come in without asking. I'll be more careful next time."

Ruby, being understanding and wise, smiled warmly at Sammy. She knew he was a good friend who didn't mean any harm. She also understood the importance of having personal space.

Even though Sammy had apologized, he wanted to learn more about personal space so he wouldn't make the same mistake again. He thought of his friend Oliver, the wise old owl who lived in the tallest tree in the forest. Everyone knew Oliver was very smart, and Sammy decided to seek his advice.

With a determined heart, Sammy set off on an adventure to meet Oliver the owl and learn all about personal space. Little did he know that this journey would teach him valuable lessons and lead to many more exciting adventures in the forest.

"Oliver," Sammy asked, "can you tell me more about personal space? I want to be an even better friend to everyone in the forest."

91

Oliver, the wise old owl, nodded his feathery head and began to explain, "You see, Sammy, personal space is like an invisible bubble around each animal. It's where they feel safe and cozy, just like their very own special hideaway. Even though we're friends, all the animals in the forest, like Ruby and Bella, need their own personal space."

Sammy listened carefully, his fluffy tail twitching with interest. He asked, "How can I show that I respect personal space, Oliver?"

Oliver hooted with wisdom and replied, "Well, Sammy, I've got some great advice for you. First, always be polite and ask if you can enter someone's home or space. Second, watch how they act and their body language. If they seem uncomfortable or move away, give them some room. And third, remember that personal space is different for everyone. What's okay for one animal might not be okay for another."

Sammy felt like a sponge soaking up all this valuable information.

He decided to put it into practice right away. He scurried over to visit his friend Bella, the busy badger known for her incredible digging and cozy dens.

"Bella," Sammy asked in his politest squirrel voice, "may I please come and visit your den? I'd love to share a fun story with you."

Bella's eyes lit up with delight. She said, "Of course, Sammy! Thank you for asking so nicely. Please, come on in."

Sammy hopped into Bella's den and settled down at the entrance. He began to tell her an exciting story about a brave squirrel on a daring adventure. Bella snuggled into her cozy den, feeling safe and appreciated. Sammy's newfound knowledge about personal space had made his friendship with Bella even stronger.

Sammy kept practicing what he'd learned. He always asked for permission and paid attention to his friends' body language. He saw that by giving them their space, his friendships grew even stronger.

One day, Sammy saw Timmy the turtle basking in the warm sun. Timmy was known for being slow and loving quiet moments in the sun.

Sammy really wanted to play tag with Timmy, but he remembered the rule about personal space. He asked Timmy, "Timmy, would you like to play tag with me?"

Timmy liked that Sammy asked in a friendly way. He thought for a moment and said, "I'd like to play, Sammy, but I'm really enjoying this quiet sun time right now. Maybe later?"

Sammy smiled and said, "Sure, Timmy. Enjoy your peaceful moment. Let me know when you're ready to play."

As Sammy walked away, he felt proud that he'd respected Timmy's personal space. He knew that being a good friend meant understanding when others needed their own time and space.

So, in the lively forest filled with all sorts of animals, Sammy learned something very important - how to give others their own space. He found out that by asking, paying attention, and understanding that everyone has different personal space, he could be an even better friend and make the forest a happier and more caring place.

Sammy's adventures continued, and he shared what he learned with all his friends. The forest became an even happier and more understanding place for everyone because of Sammy's kind heart.

The end.

Story 19

Felix the Flexible Fox

In a beautiful meadow near a calm forest, there was a young fox named Felix. Everyone in the meadow knew Felix because he was really good at moving around and doing different things. But what Felix liked the most was the idea of being flexible.

You see, life in the meadow was always bringing new surprises and tricky situations. Sometimes, the weather would suddenly change, making things very different. Other times, it was hard to find enough food to eat, and things didn't always go as planned. Felix knew that if you want to do well in a world that's always changing, you have to be flexible.

Felix's friends often asked him, "How do you stay so cool when everything is changing all the time?" Felix would smile and say, "Well, I remember that change is just a part of life, like a new adventure every day. Instead of getting upset, I try to learn from the changes and use them to help me grow."

So, Felix showed everyone in the meadow that being flexible, like a reed bending with the wind, could help them face any challenge that came their way. And they all learned that being flexible was not only helpful but also a fun way to make each day an exciting new adventure in the meadow.

One bright and sunny morning, while Felix was hopping and skipping across the meadow, he noticed his friend Mia the mouse struggling to reach a bunch of tasty berries. Mia was famous for her tiny size and endless energy, but today, those berries were just out of her grasp.

With a friendly smile, Felix trotted over and said, "Hey, Mia! Would you like some help getting to those yummy berries?"

Mia's eyes sparkled with thankfulness, and she replied, "Oh, Felix, that would be fantastic! But how can you help? You're so much bigger than me."

Felix bent down and carefully reached out his paw, gently plucking the juiciest berries and creating a little pile for Mia to enjoy. Mia's happiness was so infectious that they both had a berry feast, giggling and munching away.

As they sat together under the warm sun, Mia said, "Felix, you're so adaptable and flexible. I wish I could be like that."

Felix chuckled and replied, "Mia, flexibility isn't just about being able to stretch and bend; it's also about being open to changes and finding clever ways to solve problems in life. Anyone can learn to be flexible."

Determined to understand more about flexibility, Mia decided to have a chat with their wise friend, Oscar the owl. Oscar was

famous for his knowledge and wisdom, and Mia believed he could teach her a lot about the art of being flexible.

"Oscar," Mia began with curiosity, "can you teach me more about flexibility? I really want to learn how to adapt to changes and face life's challenges."

Oscar, the wise owl, nodded in agreement and began to explain, "Flexibility means being open to new ideas, trying different ways to do things, and not being afraid of change. It's like being a problem-solving detective when things don't go as planned."

Mia listened carefully and asked, "So, Oscar, how can I become more flexible?"

Oscar shared his valuable wisdom, saying, "You can start by keeping your mind open and learning from everything that happens to you.

When things don't go as you expected, don't give up. Look for other ways to solve the problem, and remember that being flexible is a skill you can practice and get better at over time."

Mia thanked Oscar for his wise advice and decided to put it into practice in her everyday life. She welcomed changes and faced challenges with a positive attitude.

One sunny day, out of the blue, a rainstorm swept across the meadow, surprising all the animals. Felix and Mia had planned a fun picnic, but the rain threatened to ruin their outdoor adventure.

Felix turned to Mia and said, "Mia, I know we wanted to have a picnic, but how about we have an indoor picnic in my cozy burrow? We can still enjoy our meal, stay dry, and have a good time."

Mia agreed with a cheerful smile, and they quickly gathered their picnic goodies and headed to Felix's snug burrow. Inside, they lit a warm fire, laid out their feast, and listened to the gentle sound of raindrops on the roof.

As they sat together, Felix said, "You see, Mia, flexibility can turn unexpected changes into new and enjoyable adventures."

Mia nodded in agreement, realizing that being flexible allowed them to adapt to the situation and turn it into a fun experience.

In the weeks that followed, Mia continued to practice flexibility. When she faced obstacles or changes in her daily life, she met them with an open heart and a willingness to adapt. She discovered that by being flexible, she could find creative solutions and transform challenges into exciting opportunities.

One sunny morning, Mia noticed a group of young rabbits struggling to build a bridge across a small stream so they could reach a field of tasty clover. But their bridge kept falling apart.

Mia approached them and kindly said, "Would you like some help with building your bridge?"

The young rabbits were thrilled to accept her offer. Mia brought Felix along, and together, they put their heads together to come up with a new plan for the bridge, using strong sticks and sturdy vines.

With Felix's agility and Mia's creativity, they built a strong and reliable bridge that allowed the young rabbits to reach the clover field safely. The rabbits were grateful for their help and learned the value of flexibility from Mia and Felix.

And so, in the picturesque meadow on the edge of the serene forest, animals learned the important lesson of flexibility. They realized that by being open to change, embracing challenges, and finding creative solutions, they could thrive in an ever-changing world and create a harmonious and adaptable community.

The end.

Story 20

The Adventure of Ava the Awakened Ant

In a lively anthill nestled deep within a sunny meadow, lived a young ant named Ava. Ava was no ordinary ant; she had a remarkable talent for spotting the tiniest details and keeping her eyes wide open to the world around her. But what truly filled Ava's heart with joy was the valuable lesson of paying attention.

You see, life in the anthill was a whirlwind of activity. Ants scurried about, tirelessly carving tunnels, gathering food, and then carving even more tunnels. Yet, amidst this constant hustle and bustle, Ava had discovered a secret: by being aware of everything around her, she could uncover the hidden beauty and exciting wonders concealed within their anthill home.

One sunny morning, while Ava was carefully looking at a tiny dewdrop on a blade of grass, her friend Oscar the ant came over. Oscar was famous for being very curious and always ready for an adventure.

Oscar asked Ava, "What are you looking at, Ava? Why is that dewdrop so interesting?"

Ava smiled and said, "I'm learning that when we pay attention to even the smallest things, like this dewdrop, we can discover amazing secrets and stories right here in our anthill. It's like a treasure hunt, Oscar!"

Oscar's eyes sparkled with excitement, and he joined Ava in exploring their anthill with open eyes, ready to discover the hidden wonders that were waiting for them. And from that day on, Ava and Oscar became the best treasure hunters in their anthill, finding joy in the little things all around them.

"Hey, Ava," Oscar exclaimed with excitement, "I've heard about a secret place deep within the anthill that no one has ever explored. Do you want to go with me and find out what's there?"

Ava looked at Oscar, her eyes gleaming with anticipation, and replied, "Oscar, I'm so excited too! But before we go on our adventure, let's practice being aware. If we pay attention to all the little things around us, our journey will be even more amazing."

Oscar was intrigued by the idea and agreed to start their adventure by sharpening their awareness. Together, they examined the tiny footprints of other ants, the intricate patterns on leaves, and how the sunlight played games as it filtered through the grass.

As they ventured deeper into the anthill, they stumbled upon a hidden chamber filled with sparkling crystals that glittered like stars. Ava's eyes widened in awe, and she whispered, "Oscar, look at these beautiful crystals! They've been right here all this time, but we never noticed them before. This is the magic of paying attention."

Oscar grinned, realizing that their adventure had just begun, and it was going to be full of incredible discoveries. Hand in hand, they continued their journey, ready to uncover the many more hidden wonders that awaited them in their anthill.

Oscar was amazed and nodded in wonder when he realized that by paying attention to the things around them, he and Ava had found something truly amazing right in their own home.

Their adventures didn't stop there. Ava and Oscar made sure to be aware of everything they saw. They saw ants working busily, heard the water dropping in secret underground streams, and marveled at the ants' incredible anthill houses.

One sunny day, while they were exploring a brand-new tunnel, they found a family of ants who were in trouble. The tunnel had fallen down, and the ants were stuck inside. The family was very scared and needed help.

Ava and Oscar sprang into action! They used their special awareness to understand what was happening. They noticed a tiny hole in the tunnel that had collapsed, just big enough for them to squeeze through. Together, they guided the ant family to safety, using their awareness to show them the way through the twisty tunnels of the anthill.

The saved ant family was so grateful, and Ava explained, "It was our special awareness that helped us find the hole and save you. Being aware is like having a superpower. It can make a huge difference in our lives."

From that day forward, everyone called Ava and Oscar the "Awakened Ants." They didn't just explore their world; they also helped others see the beauty and wonder hidden in their anthill home. And their anthill became a much happier place because of it.

Their fellow ants were inspired by Ava and Oscar's awareness and started practicing it too. They began to notice the bright colors of the underground fungi, the delicate patterns of spiderwebs, and the sweet songs of crickets in the distance. The anthill changed into a magical place filled with amazement and gratefulness.

One sunny afternoon, while Ava and Oscar were basking in the warm meadow above, they spotted something truly special. The meadow was alive with activity, from busy bees to colorful wildflowers, and everything seemed to be dancing together in perfect harmony.

Ava turned to Oscar with excitement and said, "Oscar, our awareness hasn't just made our lives in the anthill better, but it's also connected us to the world above. We're a part of a big, beautiful web of life."

Oscar beamed and replied, "You're absolutely right, Ava. Being aware has opened our eyes to the amazing things around us."

And so, deep within the busy anthill in a sunny meadow, the ants discovered the important lesson of awareness. They realized that by paying attention to the little things around them, they could uncover the beauty and wonder hidden right in their own home and feel connected to the vast world beyond. The ants' lives were forever changed by their newfound awareness, and they lived happily ever after, knowing that the world was full of incredible surprises waiting to be noticed.

The end.

Bonus story 1

Milo and the Magical Music Box

Once upon a time, in a small, cozy town by the sparkling sea, there lived a young boy named Milo. Milo was a very curious boy who loved collecting strange and wonderful things. He enjoyed exploring the hidden treasures in his town's old stores. But the most special place for him was Mr. Ollivander's Antiques, a dusty shop full of amazing objects that whispered stories from long ago.

One bright and sunny day, as Milo was looking at the shelves in Mr. Ollivander's shop, he discovered a very unusual music box. It was not like any other music box he had ever seen. It had intricated, swirling designs and an air of mystery that felt like a warm hug. With great excitement, Milo turned the tiny key on the side, and something incredible happened. The music box came to life, and it filled the room with a melody that was so magical, it made Milo's heart dance with joy.

The music box came to life, and the room was bathed in a melody so lovely that it seemed like a joyful dance in Milo's heart. The music tinkled and twinkled, sounding just like the laughter of a thousand happy fairies. Milo couldn't resist swaying to the enchanting tune, feeling as if he were joining in a dance of magic and delight.

The magical music curled around Milo like a warm hug, and he just had to follow its captivating tune. It pulled him closer to discover more about this incredible music box. Mr. Ollivander, the clever shopkeeper, leaned in, and in a soft voice, he shared the music box's secrets with Milo. It was not just any treasure; it was super special, one of a kind, and its history was hidden under a big cloak of mystery. Stories from long ago said that the music box had a magical power, a power that could sweep its listener off to faraway lands filled with the most amazing wonders you can ever think of.

Milo's curiosity was like fizzy soda bubbling up inside him, and he just couldn't resist the urge to test the legend all by himself. With a determined twist, he wound the music box's key until the room was filled with its enchanting tune. And oh, what a surprise awaited him! The world around him started to shimmer and change, and in the blink of an eye, he was standing in a breathtaking, magical forest.

In this wonderful forest, the trees were tall and wise, and their leaves sparkled in shades of green and gold, just like precious gems. Colorful birds with wings that glistened like rainbows flitted and fluttered all around, and friendly creatures with eyes full of ancient wisdom came up to Milo, curious about their new friend.

As Milo ventured deeper into this magical forest, he discovered something truly amazing. The music box had given him a special gift. Now, he could understand and talk to the animals and mystical beings who lived there. He quickly became friends with a playful unicorn named Luna, a wise old owl named Oliver, and a mischievous forest sprite named Willow. Together, they embarked on incredible adventures, exploring the wonders of the enchanted forest and creating cherished memories that would last a lifetime.

Milo's newfound friends became his guides through the enchanting forest, revealing its hidden secrets and wonders. He learned about the magical healing waters of the forest, listened to the ancient tales whispered by the wise trees, and followed the secret paths leading to other mystical realms, each filled with its own enchanting marvels.

As the shiny sun said goodnight and slipped beneath the edge of the sky, Milo understood that it was time to return to his everyday world. He cradled the music box gently in his hands, and with a smile, he turned its little key again, letting the enchanting melody fill the air. In the blink of an eye, he was back in the cozy, dusty corners of Mr. Ollivander's antique shop, feeling both grateful for his magical adventure and excited for the many more curious journeys that awaited him.

Milo felt deep inside that his adventure had been something truly, truly special. He couldn't wait to tell his friends and family about all the amazing things he'd seen and done because he had learned something very, very important. The magic of the music box had touched his heart in a big way. It had shown him how fantastic it is to be curious, how wonderful friendships can be when they happen unexpectedly, and how there is no end to the amazement you can find when you follow your dreams.

Starting from that day, Milo held the music box very close to his heart. It wasn't just another item among his collectibles; it was like a magical symbol that reminded him of the amazing world out there, a world filled with wonders for those who dare to be curious.

And so, in that charming old town by the sea, Milo continued his exciting journey. He kept exploring, gathering strange and amazing things, and dreaming big dreams. He understood that every treasure he discovered could lead to a magical adventure all its own. Milo believed that as long as he stayed curious and followed his passions, there would always be more enchanting stories just waiting around the corner, eager to whisk him away to new and extraordinary places. And with a heart full of wonder, he knew that his adventures would never truly end.

The end.

Bonus story 2

The Dream Weaver's Lullaby

Once upon a time, in a tiny, snug village tucked snugly between big, green hills, there was a kind old lady named Granny Mabel. Everyone in the village loved Granny Mabel. She had a warm smile, a big heart, and a magical talent for creating wonderful dreams.

Every evening, when the sun said its goodnight to the world, Granny Mabel would sit on her porch. All around her were balls of colorful yarn and an old, well-loved weaving machine. She was known as the Dream Weaver of the village, and her special gift was to make dreams for those who needed them.

Granny Mabel's porch was a magical place. It was covered in bright flowers of every color, and a gentle breeze always seemed to whisper secrets to her. The children of the village loved to visit her porch, especially in the evenings.

"Granny Mabel, please weave us a dream tonight," they would say, their eyes filled with wonder.

Granny Mabel would nod with a twinkle in her eye and invite them to sit beside her. She would ask them, "What kind of dream would you like tonight, my dear?"

The children would close their eyes and think about the most beautiful dreams they could imagine. Some wanted to fly like birds, while others dreamed of exploring magical lands. Some wished for adventures with talking animals, while others simply wanted dreams filled with laughter and joy.

Granny Mabel would listen carefully to each child's wish and then start her old weaving machine. As the colorful yarn spun and danced, Granny Mabel's fingers moved like magic. She would weave the dreams with love, care, and a sprinkle of stardust.

When the dreams were ready, Granny Mabel would place them in small, golden bags. She would hand these precious bags to the children, who would leave her porch with smiles as big as rainbows.

One cold evening, when the sky was covered in sparkling stars like a warm, fuzzy blanket, a young girl named Emma decided to visit Granny Mabel. Emma couldn't fall asleep because her head was filled with worries and things that scared her.

Granny Mabel gave Emma a big, comforting hug and invited her to sit next to her on the porch. She handed Emma a soft ball of sparkling blue yarn.

"Close your eyes, my dear," whispered Granny Mabel, "and together, we'll create a dream that will take you on a fantastic journey."

With Granny Mabel's magical words as her guide, Emma closed her eyes and started to imagine. She saw herself in a big, enchanted forest where fireflies lit up the trees like twinkling stars. Emma even pictured herself riding on the back of a friendly dragon, going to far-off lands full of amazing wonders and secrets.

While Emma's imagination flowed, Granny Mabel's hands danced skillfully on the weaving machine. She turned colorful yarn into a dream picture, where each piece of string was a special part of the adventure.

The night was filled with the songs of crickets and the soft noise of Granny Mabel's weaving machine. Emma's worries disappeared as she got lost in the magical world they were making together.

When the dream was finished, Granny Mabel put it into Emma's hands. Emma opened her eyes, and her face lit up with amazement as she held the dream in her hands. It was a dream come true, a special gift from Granny Mabel for a fantastic adventure that night.

"Take this dream with you, dear Emma," Granny Mabel said with a warm smile. She reached out and gently placed the dream in Emma's hands. "Whenever you close your eyes and let your imagination soar, it will whisk you away to the magical forest, where fireflies light up the trees like twinkling stars. You can visit your friend, the friendly dragon, and explore the far-off lands filled with exciting adventures."

Emma's eyes widened with wonder as she held the dream close to her heart. Granny Mabel continued, "Let this dream be your special friend, guiding you through even the darkest of nights. Dreams, you see, are like little lanterns in the night sky, lighting up the path to your biggest adventures and brightest dreams. They remind us that anything is possible, and even in the quietest moments, our imaginations can take us on the grandest journeys."

With a grateful nod, Emma hugged the dream tightly and whispered, "Thank you, Granny Mabel, for this magical gift."

Granny Mabel's smile grew even warmer as she patted Emma's shoulder. "You're welcome, my dear. Now, off you go and enjoy your dream adventure whenever your heart desires. Just remember, dreams are always there to show you the way to wonderful places and incredible stories waiting to be told."

And so, Emma went to bed that night with her heart full of hope, knowing that Granny Mabel's special dream would always be there to light up her dreams and take her on exciting journeys.

Emma hugged Granny Mabel tightly, her smile shining as brightly as the stars above. With the dream tucked safely in her heart, she headed back home and slipped into a peaceful sleep, where her imagination danced with magic.

In that snug little village, nestled among the gentle hills, Granny Mabel carried on weaving dreams. She touched the hearts of those who needed a little extra magic in their lives, reminding them that even in their dreams, the most extraordinary adventures awaited them.

Granny Mabel's porch was the most magical place in the village, and she was the kindest, most wonderful Dream Weaver anyone could ever imagine. And so, in the little village nestled between the green hills, Granny Mabel's love and dreams filled the hearts of all, making every night a special adventure for the children and a dream come true for everyone who knew her.

As the night wrapped its cozy blanket around the village, the Dream Weaver's lullaby of dreams and starlight sang everyone to sleep. They drifted off, knowing that in their dreams, there was a world full of endless wonders waiting for them.

The end.

Bonus story 3

The Little Star's Big Dream

Once upon a time, in the big, glittering night sky, lived a tiny star named Stella. Stella was special, but not like the other stars. She didn't twinkle super brightly or light up the sky like her starry friends. Stella was a humble and gentle star, and sometimes she felt a bit small and not very important compared to the other dazzling stars all around her.

One peaceful and quiet night, as Stella gazed up at the sky, she spotted a shooting star zooming across the heavenly painting above. Stella let out a gentle sigh and quietly told herself, "Oh, how I wish I could do something special like that." And so, her wish began an amazing adventure for little Stella.

But little did Stella know that she wasn't alone in the quiet sky. Luna, the kind and gentle moon, had overheard Stella's heartfelt wish. Luna was a believer in dreams and wanted to help Stella's wish come true.

The very next night, Luna wrapped a delicate moonbeam around Stella and whispered, "Hold on tightly, Stella. We're embarking on an extraordinary adventure."

And so, Stella and Luna soared through the night sky, their luminous journey taking them past radiant planets, a dance with the twinkling constellations, and even a thrilling race alongside comets. Stella felt a thrill and excitement she had never experienced before.

As they journeyed further and deeper into the cosmos, they came upon a dark and lonely corner of the sky. In that dimly lit space, they found a faded and dejected star named Nova. Nova had lost not only its shine but also its hope.

Luna, with her gentle and soothing moonlight, reached out and touched Nova's heart. "You are not alone," Luna spoke softly. "Stella and I are here to brighten your night."

With Luna's warm encouragement and Stella's gentle glow, Nova began to shimmer once more. The three stars filled the dark corner with a radiant and beautiful light, creating a brand-new constellation that sparkled like a cosmic jewel.

Stella came to realize that she didn't have to be the brightest star in the sky to make a difference. Just like Luna and Nova had done for her, she could bring light and hope to others.

With a heart filled with gratitude, Stella returned to her place in the night sky. She no longer felt small or insignificant. She understood that every star, no matter how big or small, had a unique purpose. Her purpose was to bring light and hope to those who needed it.

From that night on, Stella shone with newfound confidence. She no longer compared herself to the other stars but focused on spreading her gentle glow to every corner of the sky.

And so, Stella the little star, Luna the gentle moon, and Nova the once-faded star continued to light up the night sky, each in their own unique and special way. Together, they taught the world that even the tiniest star could have the most significant impact when they followed their heart and shared their light with others.

In the end, they proved that in the vastness of the universe, it's not about how brightly you shine but how much light and love you bring to those around you. And they lived happily ever after, lighting up the night with their gentle, radiant glow.

As Stella, Luna, and Nova continued their nightly adventures, they made new friends among the celestial wonders. They met Twinkle, a mischievous star who loved to play hide-and-seek among the clouds, and Spark, a star with a fiery personality who could create dazzling fireworks displays in the sky.

One night, a meteor shower painted streaks of silver across the heavens. Stella, with her newfound confidence, decided to join in the fun. Luna and Nova cheered her on as she streaked across the sky, leaving a trail of stardust that sparkled like magic.

The other stars marveled at Stella's newfound talent. They realized that even the gentlest star could surprise everyone with hidden abilities. Stella's heart swelled with happiness as she saw the admiration in their twinkling eyes.

One chilly night, a tiny astronaut named Alex gazed up at the night sky through a telescope. To his surprise, he noticed the unique constellation formed by Stella, Luna, and Nova. It looked like a bright, shining heart in the sky. Alex smiled and made a wish on a shooting star, thanking the stars above for their beauty and inspiration.

Word of the special constellation spread across the land, and people came from far and wide to see it. They brought their dreams and wishes, believing that the constellation would help them come true.

Stella, Luna, and Nova felt a warm glow of happiness in their hearts as they saw how their light had touched the lives of others. They realized that they had become a symbol of hope, love, and dreams for people all around the world.

And so, every night, Stella, Luna, and Nova continued to shine their gentle, radiant glow, not only lighting up the night sky but also the hearts of those who looked up and believed in the magic of the stars.

As they watched over the world, they knew that no matter how small or humble they might seem, they had a unique and special purpose in the grand tapestry of the universe. And in their quiet way, they brought light, hope, and dreams to the hearts of all who dared to dream.

The end.

Other Pillow Tales

Published autumn 2023

Available on Amazon.com

Printed in Great Britain
by Amazon

44618532R00069